sexy
STRANGER

KENDALL RYAN

Sexy Stranger
Copyright © 2017 Kendall Ryan

Copy Editing and Formatting by
Pam Berehulke

Cover Design by
Okay Creations

Photography by
Sara Eirew

All rights reserved. No part of this book may be reproduced or transmitted in any form without written permission of the author, except by a reviewer who may quote brief passages for review purposes only.

This book is a work of fiction. Names, characters, places, and incidents are either the product of the author's imagination or are used fictitiously.

About the Book

Luke Wilder knows the lovely stranger doesn't belong the second she struts into his sleepy little town. She's a city girl who won't stay longer than it takes to get her fancy foreign car repaired—which is why he should ignore his powerful need to make her notice him. It's just that the moment she opens her smart mouth and gives it back as good as she gets, he wants to swap a whole lot more with her than insults.

Charlotte Freemont instantly dislikes the rude redneck stranger she finds herself stuck with. Too bad he's as hot as sin, and just as tempting. On the run from her messy past, she's not there to get tangled up with a man, even one as hard to resist as the hotheaded Luke. But when he gives her a private tour of his craft whiskey distillery, their attraction ignites, and Luke seizes the chance to show her there's a whole lot more to him than the rough, rugged side she sees.

When he finally learns her secret, will it shatter his trust in her? Or do they have a chance to create a whole new blend?

Chapter One

Luke

There was nothing quite like watching an out-of-towner get their first taste of Shady Grove. It didn't happen too often. In my experience, you were either from here or you'd never heard of the place.

The second I saw her walk through the door of What the Cluck, the local family-style restaurant, I knew she didn't belong, and so did everyone else whose head turned in her direction. The ones who didn't notice right away surely did when they heard her heels clicking across the worn wooden floors. Even the hum of the gossip mill couldn't drown out the sound of stilettos on pine.

My first impression of her was lean curves, dark shiny hair, and a round peach of an ass that was begging to be grabbed, spanked, and bitten. Then my sister leaned over and whispered in my ear, causing my dirty mind to screech to an unwelcome halt.

"I heard her car broke down."

I acknowledged Molly's comment with a nod. Instead of focusing on the whispers of the people around me, I found myself more intrigued with the expression on the newcomer's face. It was quite a face, after all. Her big blue eyes were wide with bewilderment, her pretty pink lips pursed as she tried to flag down one of the waitresses busily rushing by her. Her cute little nose wrinkled in confusion when a passing waitress finally called out, "Seat yourself, honey!"

I quickly dropped my attention when I realized the one open seat in the place was directly across from me.

So much for quiet observation.

I could certainly appreciate a beautiful woman, but the last thing I was interested in was getting mixed up with a passerby's drama—despite how sexy her legs looked as she walked toward the table. This chick would be gone and forgotten before sundown, just like everyone else who didn't belong here.

My twin brother was seated across from my sister, and about to be shoulder to shoulder with the newbie. Duke smirked when I looked up. The unspoken conversation we had during the time it took her to sit next to him was totally inappropriate for Sunday lunch. It basically consisted of my brother silently saying, *I'm gonna try and hit that*, and me replying, *Don't always think with your dick*.

The connection between us was twenty-nine years strong. I didn't need him to tell me what he was thinking. We'd been doing the same song and dance since we'd realized that our dicks could be used for more than just pissing. It wasn't that I didn't think about sex, just that Duke thought about it a whole lot more. And it had landed him in a few prickly situations over the years. Last thing I wanted was to clean up another mess of his.

Duke wasn't the only curious one. I looked over at my sister and saw she was champing at the bit to find out about the stranger. There was no stopping Molly when she wanted to get to the bottom of something. She'd been the most inquisitive child I'd ever met, and at twenty-four, she hadn't stopped with her quest for the truth. If she were a cat, she would have burned through all nine of her lives by now.

"Hi," she said no sooner than the brunette was seated at our table and unfolding her napkin. "I'm Molly Wilder." She reached across the table, practically shoving her hand in the poor girl's face.

I watched as the awkwardness unfolded and tried hard not to laugh at it all.

"Oh," the stranger said, staring at my sister's hand for a moment. "We're doing this." She placed her hand in Molly's and mustered up a smile. "I'm Charlotte."

"Welcome. These are my brothers, Duke and Luke." Molly didn't wait to dive right into the interrogation. "What brings you to our fine little town?"

She released Charlotte's hand when I elbowed her slightly in the ribs, a warning to tone it down. When she side-eyed me, I simply sat back in my chair and shook my head, then tugged my weathered A&M ball cap down a bit to shield me from it. There was no stopping Molly's inquisition at this point, and Duke would probably hit on Charlotte before the biscuits were brought to the table. I knew I should have skipped today.

Like it was even an option.

Sunday lunch with my family was set in stone. Ever since our mother left when I was seven, the Wilder family had spent Sunday mornings at the Lutheran church and dined on fried chicken directly afterward. In fact, everything in this place was set in stone. Every day had a purpose, and every purpose had an end goal. There was routine and order, just the way I liked it.

What I didn't like was a disruption. Much like the one sitting across the farmhouse table from me. No, the pretty brunette with TOURIST practically stamped on her forehead was a disruption wrapped in distraction and dipped in temptation. She'd already hooked my brother with her good looks and my sister with her mystery. And there I was, caught in the middle.

"There's something wrong with my car," Charlotte told Molly. "And apparently, I have to wait until tomorrow to have it checked out."

"That's too bad." Molly gave her a sympathetic look. "So, you'll be here for a few days?"

"Oh, I hope not," Charlotte said, as if spending time in Shady Grove, Texas, was the worst thing she'd ever heard of. "Hopefully, it's a quick fix."

"Duke's pretty good with cars," Molly said, casting a stare across the table. "Maybe he could take a look."

"Yeah," he said with a grin that bounced from Molly to Charlotte. "I could get up under that hood. Take a look."

"I think I'll pass," Charlotte said without missing a beat or letting Duke's charms get the better of her.

I couldn't help the laugh that managed to break from between my pursed lips when she gave him the old *thanks, but no thanks*. I loved it when a woman gave my brother an ego check. Didn't happen too often, so I let myself enjoy the moment.

"Your loss, sweetheart," Duke said, clearly taken aback by her directness.

"I wasn't trying to sound like a bitch or anything." Charlotte gave him a tight smile. "I just . . . it's an Audi. It's probably really complicated, and a trained professional is probably better suited. I don't know that you'd be able to help me."

It was one thing for her to shoot a man down because she wasn't interested romantically, but it was quite another to shoot down his mechanical skills. Duke, like every other guy in this town, knew how to fix a car.

Even a fancy car like hers.

"So much for not sounding like a bitch," I said.

"Excuse me?" She quickly looked at me.

"You heard me." I sat up straight in my chair. "He could fix your car just fine," I assured her.

"Well, excuse me for not wanting some cowboy to poke around under the hood of my hundred-thousand-dollar car." She looked back at Duke. "No offense."

"None taken." A small smile played on his lips as he sat back and crossed his arms over his chest.

"You're just going to take it?" I asked him, confused that Duke was bowing out so easily.

"You got this," he said, giving me a nod.

I didn't know what game he was playing, but if he wasn't going to set this woman straight, I sure would. "Just because we live in Texas, we're all cowboys?"

"I just assumed. But if the boot fits," she said with a smirk, her agitation now clearly directed at me.

Which was fine. I could take it. "You know what they say about making assumptions. And you're from where? Wait."

I paused and took a second to turn my ball cap around. I wanted to make sure I was looking this snooty woman in the eye when I gave her the reality check she clearly needed. Her gaze flicked from me to Duke as the realization that we were twins sank in, but I wasn't in the mood to discuss just how much we looked alike.

"Let me guess," I said. "LA?"

"New York."

"Ah." I nodded. "Makes complete sense. I'm surprised you can even sit there, what with the stick up your ass and all. You know, because everyone from New York has one up theirs."

The oohs and aahs that came from the nearby patrons listening in on our conversation were deafening.

"Wow," Charlotte replied with a look of complete calm.

I'll be the first to admit, I was kind of impressed that

she wasn't more rattled. Hell, maybe even a little turned on. Wasn't every day you met a woman who could give as good as she could get. I thought for sure she'd get up and storm out like the spoiled brat I'd pegged her for.

"I shouldn't have assumed that you were all cowboys." She gave me a smug smile as she shook her head. "You're clearly just an asshole."

I'd never seen a woman so manicured and polished and cleaned up, it made me want to get her all dirty. And that sassy streak that ran a mile wide? Fuck, that just made me want to put her on her knees and show her who was boss.

Chapter Two

Charlotte

Never in my life had I met anyone more arrogant than the man sitting across from me. And that was really saying something, considering the high-society assholes I'd been surrounded with my entire life.

Didn't matter one bit to me that his shoulders were broad and he looked like he worked with his hands. I didn't let the image of him tossing hay bales or shoveling dirt pop into my head, or whatever it was that "not cowboys" did. The perfectly sculpted arms revealed by the short sleeves of his T-shirt didn't distract me. Not one damn bit.

"Takes one to know one, sweetheart," he said, narrowing his eyes on mine.

Now that his hat was out of the way, I could see the almost evergreen color of his eyes plain and clear. Or if I really wanted an up-close look, I could glance over at his twin brother sitting next to me. They might have been the most identical twins I'd ever seen—from their green eyes to the slope of their noses, right down to the dimples they both had on each cheek. The two were practically carbon copies. If I weren't so annoyed by the one sitting across from me, I might have cozied up to the idea of spending a little time with them while I was stuck in this town, because the sexiness factor was definitely doubled too.

"I just came here to eat," I finally said, wanting to end the pointless argument.

He tugged his hat back around. "Me too."

Our conversation ended there. The glaring, however, continued for the next several minutes.

I took a deep breath and tried not to let his arrogance get the best of me. The only problem was that he was the sexiest man I'd ever seen in real life. They didn't make men like him in New York, all rugged and rough around the edges.

"All right, folks," the waitress said, finally stopping at our table. "Can I get ya some drinks, or just sweet tea all around?"

"I'll take a water with lemon," I said as the Wilders all nodded for iced tea.

The waitress nodded. "Yes, ma'am."

"And can I get a menu?"

As soon as the question was out of my mouth, the waitress and everyone within earshot snickered.

I was confused. This was a restaurant, right?

"Lunch is up on the board." The waitress turned to point at a chalkboard on the wall. "What you see is what you get." She smiled and left to check on another table.

"It's family-style," Molly explained.

"What does that mean?"

"One big meal brought out all in big bowls. All served at once."

"Oh." I finally realized what she meant. "Like Thanksgiving."

"Exactly!"

Not that any of my Thanksgiving dinners had been served that way. My family always had a fully catered meal with some fanciful version of turkey and stuffing. I imagined this particular dinner was going to be more like what I saw on television. Happy families, one big bowl of mashed potatoes, and smiles all around. Definitely not like the dinners in my memories.

Family-style wasn't in my vocabulary. And more than that, I was used to my privacy, not having to fight for elbow room and listen to other people's private conversations.

I flagged down the waitress as she passed by with a tray of biscuits. "Excuse me, but do you have a booth, or maybe just a private table in back? It's been a hell of a day, and—"

She tucked a loose lock of hair back into her braid. "I'm going to take a wild guess and wager you're not from around here."

What does that have to do with anything?

My gaze wandered back to the hottie across from me. He was smirking.

"Does this make you uncomfortable?" he asked. "Sitting close to me?"

I looked back to the waitress for help, but she was

already gone.

"I'm not uncomfortable," I said, straightening my posture.

His eyebrows jumped up as he studied me. "You look uncomfortable."

Realizing that my spine was ramrod straight and my hands were fisted in my lap, I huffed out a sigh.

A few moments later, platters generously piled with home-cooked food were delivered, and those seated around me wasted no time in loading up their plates.

"You're not going to eat?" Duke asked, leaning over to inspect my plate.

And this was why I wanted a private table. I didn't want someone checking on my progress like I was a finicky toddler who needed supervising. I didn't generally eat carbs, or things that were deep-fried in lard.

"I am eating," I told him, forking up one of the beans on my plate. "These green beans are delicious."

"Probably because they're cooked in bacon," the hottie said, his first words since the meal had started. "So,

I hope you're into fat," he added with a smirk.

Not wanting to give him a bit of satisfaction, I bit into the green bean and smiled as I slowly used my lips to pull it from the fork. I didn't miss the way his eyes widened as I ate. I learned a long time ago via *Clueless* that drawing attention to your mouth was always a surefire way to garner a man's attention. *Bacon fat be damned.*

"I am, actually," I said. "Makes it slide down easier."

I watched with delight as he swallowed hard. *Serves you right, pal.*

I wasn't sure exactly why I was so happy that he was caught up in my little performance, but it pleased me and stoked the small fire I could feel burning deep in my stomach when I looked at him. It was too bad he was such a jerk and that I'd sworn off men for the time being. We could have had a lot of fun together.

"You know you want some of my chicken," Luke said, his voice low and teasing.

I hated the shiver that raced along my spine. "I do not want your chicken."

"It's okay. You can have some, duchess."

Duchess? I wasn't sure where he'd gotten the nickname until I realized he probably had me pegged for a spoiled little rich brat. To anyone who didn't know the truth, that's probably what I looked like. But in my heart, it wasn't who I was.

Which was exactly why I'd fled and left everything behind.

Once I'd picked my plate clean of salad and green beans, I stood up without a word and went to the register to pay, and then hurried out the door. This entire meal had been a disaster, and I wasn't even close to full.

"Charlotte," a voice called out as I walked down the sidewalk toward the auto repair shop.

I turned to find Molly chasing after me, leaving her brothers waiting by the front door of the restaurant. I stopped and let her catch up.

"I'm real sorry about Luke," she said. "He's usually not so uptight. I'm not sure what got into him."

In the sunlight, I could see her resemblance to her

brothers. The same sun-bleached brown hair and sweet smile. But where the twins' eyes were green, hers were brown, and she had no dimples. She was a pretty girl with a good disposition, probably the kind of person I could—or at least, should—be friends with if the circumstances were different.

"It's all right," I told her. "You don't have to apologize for him." Looking over her shoulder, I sneaked a quick glance at the jerk. Our eyes locked for a moment, but I quickly looked back to Molly. "He's a grown-up. He should be able to handle himself."

"I just wanted to welcome you to town. Hope you don't think we're all assholes," she said with a chuckle, and I smiled back.

"I don't."

"Good." She placed a hand on my shoulder. "I hope I see you around," she added before hurrying back in her brothers' direction.

As nice as making a new friend would be, I was hoping my time in Shady Grove was close to over.

•••

I'd been in this little town all of an hour, and already it felt like hell. After my car had coasted into Shady Grove making an awful screeching noise, I'd parked it at the only gas station I saw, which was also an auto repair shop. Unfortunately, a sign posted on the door read CLOSED FOR LUNCH.

"I'm sorry, what?" I said to the attendant behind the counter. I'd been so happy when I got back from my own lunch and found that the little repair shop had reopened. My relief was quickly dashed by the woman running the register.

"Wayne's out today," she said.

I assumed she was referring to the Wayne of WAYNE'S AUTO REPAIR, as the sign on the outside of the building stated.

"Could you call him?" I asked as politely as I could.

"It's Sunday."

"Okay . . ." I waited for a better explanation, and when it wasn't forthcoming, asked, "Why does that matter?"

She chuckled. "Wayne doesn't work on Sunday."

"I'll pay him to work on Sunday."

The one thing I had been sure to pack when I left New York was the black AmEx card my parents had given me. They might not be my favorite people at the moment, but I had no problem spending their money if I had to.

"Honey," she said, leaning over to rest her forearms on the counter that separated us. Her graying blond hair was set in curls from what I assumed was a perm, and the realization of just how out of place I was started to set in. "Let me put it this way. Wayne doesn't work on Sunday because he's probably been drinking since Friday. He'd be useless today. And the Longhorns kick off in about fifteen minutes. There's a better chance of that pretty little car of yours fixing itself than getting Wayne to come in today."

"Maggie," I said after glancing at her name tag. "Are there any other mechanics in this town that work on Sunday?"

"I'm sorry." She shook her head and offered her sympathy with a half smile. "Wayne's the only mechanic in town."

"That's just great."

I rubbed my hands over my face, hoping that maybe this was all just a dream. When I opened my eyes and the fluorescent lighting and Maggie's apathetic face greeted me, I knew my reality was much worse than I'd thought.

"What should I do?" I finally asked.

"There's a little bed and breakfast—the Willow Inn—a few blocks that way." She pointed out the window of the station. "Maybe get a hot shower," she suggested. "Relax."

I nodded, trying not to cry out of utter frustration. The last hour had been eventful, and not in a good way, and now it looked like I was spending the night in Shady Grove whether I liked it or not.

"Wayne comes in early, so as soon as you get up in the morning, you come on down. He'll help you out."

"Thanks," I muttered, unable to muster up a smile.

Not that she'd helped much, anyway.

I started to push through the door and set off for the B&B she'd recommended, and then glanced back in her direction.

"How far of a walk is it to the inn?" I looked down at my cute suede booties with their five-inch heels. "Should I call an Uber?"

"A what?"

"You know, like a driving service? Or maybe a cab?"

Maggie's laugh came up from deep in her chest. When she recognized that I wasn't amused, she paused and composed herself. "Oh, bless your heart. We don't have anything like that here. Besides, it's only a half mile down to the Willow," she assured me.

I thanked her with a nod and saved the eye roll for when I was alone in the parking lot and gathering my belongings from my car. No Starbucks, no Uber, and not a mechanic in sight.

What kind of hell did I stumble into?

..."Their names are Luke and Duke," I told Valentina over the phone. After I'd checked in and gotten settled in my room, I'd wandered downstairs and found a comfy chair in a secluded spot of the living room. The sun was starting to set on this day, and tomorrow couldn't come fast enough.

"Seriously?" she said with a chuckle. It was the same thought I'd had when I'd pieced it all together on my walk home. "Twins named Luke and Duke. That's so country."

"Isn't it?" I laughed.

The finish line was in my sights, and the thought of being in this town for any longer than I had to was nauseating. Besides that, I had a new life to start living. When I'd packed up and started off on this adventure, I told myself it was a new beginning. But at the moment, it felt like I was in a purgatory of open cornfields and hot, arrogant assholes with muscles to the moon and back.

"Just breathe for me. You'll be here in a couple of days, tops."

"I know," I said, feigning enthusiasm.

It's not that I wasn't excited about getting to Valentina's—she was the only person who'd ever really understood exactly who I was. No, it was the fifteen hundred miles that stood between here and there that had me down.

I checked my reflection in the antique mirror hanging on the wall. The demands and expectations I'd endured had left a serious mark on me, and had apparently started me down the path of early aging. Twenty-eight was far too young to feel so beat down.

Nothing a little West Coast sunshine won't clear up.

With my fresh start so close, I hated the idea of any more delays.

"It's too bad one of them was such a jerk," I added. "They're not too bad to look at."

I hadn't been able to shake the image of Luke staring at me. As annoying as he was, he'd ignited a spark of attraction that I hadn't felt in a very long time. It had to be a result of my last relationship, the one where I was underappreciated and often ignored. My libido had apparently taken Luke's aggression as attention and decided to fire back up.

"You would find the only hot twins in the middle of nowhere." She chuckled. "I can't wait for you to get here. It's been too long."

"I saw you a week ago," I said. "You know, right before I walked out on . . ." I searched for the right word, but there were so many that would finish the sentence. *Everything. My parents. An entire guest list full of people. My guaranteed future of privilege.*

"Don't even say it," Valentina said. "You're moving on, remember? Moving forward."

"Well, I'm not moving forward at the moment," I reminded her. "Currently, I'm stuck."

"Yeah, but you're stuck in a town with hot twins, so quit complaining."

"Yeah, yeah." I rolled my eyes at the smirk I was sure she had on her face. "Fingers crossed my car is fixed tomorrow, and I can get back to moving on."

"Fingers crossed," she repeated before we said our good-byes.

I hung up my phone and placed it on the arm of the chair before picking up the magazine I'd started reading before Valentina called.

"Did I hear that you met the Wilders?"

Opal, the front desk clerk who'd checked me in, interrupted me right before I found out exactly what happened between the latest celebrity-couple split. I looked up from the pages and found her standing in the archway that separated the lobby from the living room.

"I did," I said. "Wasn't impressed."

"They're good people. You must have caught them on a bad day."

"Maybe. I did like Molly. And Duke wasn't terrible."

"It's a shame what they've been through."

She turned to walk away, but I was intrigued.

"Wait . . . What have they been through?"

Opal stopped and turned back to face me, her eyes full of sadness. "Their momma ran out on them when they were just babies. And their daddy may as well have.

He really tried, but the man just couldn't put down the bottle."

"That's terrible."

"Those boys had to grow up real fast. Taking care of Molly, running the family business. It was a lot to handle, but they've done the best they could."

My heart clenched as I thought about younger versions of Luke and Duke trying to take care of Molly.

Opal gave me a smile. "Anyway, I didn't mean to bring down your evening. Just thought you might want to give them a fair shake before you wrote them off. And their full names are Lucas and Daniel," she added. "Luke and Duke are just nicknames they picked up along the way."

Chapter Three

Luke

"Morning, Wayne," I said as I stepped inside the repair shop bright and early Monday morning, greeting the old bastard with as much enthusiasm as I could muster. I knew he was about to screw me on the price of a new hose for the Chevy. Damn truck had been in my family for two generations now, and was showing her age.

"Where ya been?" he asked, pulling his head out from under the hood of a fancy foreign car. "I've had your part waiting since Friday."

Sleek lines, perfect curves ... the car had to be Charlotte's. The brazen little minx had been on my mind since my run-in with her yesterday. Wanting to avoid a repeat performance, I came to the garage early to pick up my part. Didn't peg her as an early riser.

"I got tied up with a leak in one of the drums," I told him. "The entire place was a mess before we found it. Took me and Duke all weekend to get it cleaned up."

"That's a damn shame," Wayne said. "I hate it when good liquor gets spilled."

"You and me both."

It was more about the dollars that were spilled than anything. Duke and I were so close to being in the black that we could practically taste the profits. It would be a nice change since our father had done his best to run Wilder Whiskey into the ground.

"Whatcha got here?" I asked, walking over to take a peek under the hood. I thought I knew the answer, but damn it if I didn't ask.

What was it about this girl that had me so curious? I knew enough about her to know that I didn't particularly enjoy her company, but I hadn't been able to shake those blue eyes from my head. Or the sweet curve of her ass as she walked down the sidewalks I'd practically worn out over the years.

It's because she's shiny and new, dumbass.

Charlotte was the first fresh blood we'd had in this town in a long time. My ex-girlfriend was the last, and I always hoped she would stay that way. The last thing I needed was a repeat performance of that shit show. I knew for damn sure I couldn't handle it.

"Something I never thought I'd see in this place." He moved over to give me room and pointed at the engine. "You know anything about Audis?"

"I know they cost way too much," I said with a smirk. "A hundred grand, I think." I tried to recall exactly what Charlotte had spouted off at What the Cluck.

"Well, shit," Wayne said. "I'd better put on some gloves." He wiped one of his greasy hands down the front of his overalls.

"It was actually a hundred twenty thousand," an all-too-familiar sarcastic voice offered. "If you want to be specific."

"I'd say you paid too much," I said, turning to find the early riser.

Charlotte stood there in a simple white T-shirt, ripped-up denim jeans, and Converse tennis shoes. At first glance, it almost looked like she fit in here in our small town, but I had a pretty good idea that her outfit cost more than the Chevy part I was here to pick up.

"Good thing I didn't pay for it," she said with a

smirk.

"I figured."

"What's that supposed to mean?"

She crossed her arms across her body, inadvertently shoving a pretty spectacular set of tits up even more than they already perkily sat. The deep vee of her T-shirt wasn't hiding much, and I was appreciative of that.

I looked over at Wayne. He was pretty appreciative of the view too.

"Are you saying that I couldn't buy myself a car like that?" The steam rolling off her was just as sexy as the cleavage.

"Relax, Charlie," I said, feeling my cock twitch behind the zipper of my Levi's. The hold this girl had on my attention was as frustrating as hell. "I'm not saying that. I just figured that it was a gift."

"Oh, so you were assuming. You know what they say about that?" She laughed, repeating my question from the day before.

"You're right." I held up my hands in surrender. "It

was wrong. I apologize."

The satisfied smile on her face was enough to earn my apology. In fact, a string of ideas ran through my head about all the ways I could earn a few more of those smiles. I'd use a whole lot more than my words. I'd start with my mouth and hands, and then work down to the part of my body that was currently bogarting more than its fair share of my blood supply.

"Glad we could work that out." She breezed by me and extended her hand to Wayne. "I'm Charlotte Freemont. You must be Wayne."

"I am," he said, grabbing her hand with his greasy paw.

Both Wayne and Charlotte dropped their gaze to the connection between them, and I couldn't help but laugh. One was mortified that he'd forgotten about the grease, and the other had probably never been dirtier in her entire life.

"Oh, this is great," I said, leaning up against one of the other cars that Wayne had in the garage. All I needed was popcorn.

"I'm real sorry." Wayne quickly pulled a clean-ish rag from his back pocket and handed it to her.

"It's fine." Charlotte frowned as she swiped at the grease on her hand. She glanced back at me, and I sensed she was doing her best to rein in that stick-up-her-ass New York attitude. "Just tell me you can fix my car."

"I can," Wayne said proudly.

"That's great." She beamed at him as she returned his rag. "Today?"

"Well . . ." Wayne shoved the rag in the back pocket of his overalls and rubbed a hand on his neck. "'Bout that . . ."

"Come on," she pleaded. "I'll pay you extra if you have it done today. I really need to get out of here. I'm supposed to be in LA."

Of course she is.

Wayne shook his head. "Honey, even if I wanted to, I don't have the part I need."

"Where is it?"

"On its way from Amarillo. Should be here tomorrow. Wednesday at the latest."

"So, Wednesday."

"Not quite. Then I have to put the part in." He glanced skyward as he considered. "With this new engine component, it'll probably take me a while, and then I have to put the whole thing back together. Maybe Friday."

"FML." She let out a huff and rolled her eyes.

"Oh, come on, Charlie," I said, hoping to defuse the tension. "This place isn't that bad." That statement in itself earned me a glare.

"It's Charlotte," she reminded me.

I knew exactly what her name was, so I just shrugged.

"You seriously can't have it done any faster?" she asked Wayne after she finished shooting daggers in my direction.

I knew as well as Wayne that if he really wanted to, he could have her car done by Wednesday. I could see the dollar signs in his eyes. If he stretched this job out long enough, he could charge a pretty penny for labor. Maybe it would serve her right for owning such an expensive car. There was nothing modest about it and clearly screamed she had money to burn.

"You can work faster than that," I told Wayne, stepping up by her side. "Just because you can take till Friday doesn't mean you have to."

"What are you doing?" Charlotte frowned at me, her confusion now laced with agitation.

"Helping you out." I flashed her a grin. *See, I can be civil. Helpful, even.*

"I don't need your help," she snapped. "I can buy my own damn cars, and I can surely negotiate a deal to get them fixed."

"I just thought—" I started to tell her that I knew a guy in Austin who could have the part in and installed well before Friday, but the girl just couldn't keep her mouth shut.

"I can take care of myself. I have a degree in marketing from Yale," she spat out. "And my family runs one of the largest firms in New York City. Thanks for the offer, but no thanks."

"Okay then." I hesitated for a moment, not wanting to lose the cool I'd been so desperately trying to keep. She wasn't making it easy. I had a business to run, and the last thing I needed was to get mixed up in her drama.

"Thanks for the part, Wayne." I gave him a nod as I grabbed the hose off the counter by the door. "Send me a bill."

I didn't even bother looking at Charlotte. If she wanted to take care of herself, she could do just that.

• • •

"Son of a bitch," I muttered, trying to get the new hose into place. After the third try, I tossed it on the ground and stepped away from the Chevy. Frustrated, I kicked up some gravel from the driveway as I paced alongside the rusty old truck and slapped a hand on the fender.

"Easy there," my brother said, easing up to me like I was a wild beast. "Take a breath. It's not the truck's fault."

"It kind of is. Goddamn thing is so old, and

everything is bent out of shape in it."

"Kind of like you right now." He cuffed my shoulder. "Especially the old part."

"Two fucking minutes older than you," I said, flipping him off. Charlotte might have been good at pushing my buttons, but Duke was an expert.

"What crawled up your ass this early?" He picked up the discarded hose and walked over to take a look under the hood for himself.

"Just one of those days. Weeks, actually. First, the leaky drum, and now this," I huffed. "And don't even get me started on Miss New York."

"Ah," Duke said as he wiggled the hose into place. "That explains it all. Lady's got your tail in a twist."

"The lady does not."

"Mm-hmm." He chuckled. "I'm sure you're really this mad over the same shit we deal with all the time. We're always fixing this truck or a broken part of the pisstillery," he said using the pet name he'd come up with for our non-profitable business.

"Yeah, I know." I sighed. "Maybe that's the problem. I'm sick of this shit."

"No, you're not," he shot back. "You're the only one in the family that actually believes we can make something out of this place."

I looked around the property, taking stock of what exactly we had—a decent farmhouse, a couple of sheds, and a fully restored barn that housed the distillery. All on a nice piece of acreage.

Duke gave me a pat on the back before he shut the hood of the Chevy. "And I didn't want to say this because I hate giving you any more of an ego boost than I have to, but that last batch we pulled was actually pretty damn good."

I grinned back at him. "It was good, wasn't it?"

"Yeah, it was. I know it's not all of this getting your goat," he said, throwing his hands out. "If Miss New York is really getting under your skin that much, I suggest you either fuck her, or go help Wayne get her car fixed and get her the hell out of town. You and I both know that only one of us can be riled up at a time, and I'm not very good at keeping my composure."

Fuck her? Was that what I really wanted? It had to be. Maybe we could take our hostility and turn it into something a little more fun.

God, I hated when my brother was the smart one. I usually wore that hat.

"Maybe you're right," I admitted with a shake of my head.

"You're goddamn right I am," he said, gloating. "So, what are you going to do about it?"

Chapter Four

Charlotte

"Let's start over," I said, trying not to think about the sexy-as-hell country boy who'd just stormed out of the repair shop.

Sure, he was just trying to help, but the second he decided that I wasn't capable of handling this situation on my own, I snapped. Now he was gone, and I was here negotiating a deal with the grease monkey.

"I need this car fixed as soon as possible. You and I both know I don't belong here," I said, and Wayne nodded in agreement. "Can you please help me out?"

"I'll put your car at the top of the list," he finally agreed. "I'll aim for Wednesday, but I'm charging extra for the rush job."

"I wouldn't expect anything less," I said with a smile.

When he reached out his hand to seal the deal, I hesitated. Mine were still greasy from our first handshake.

When I didn't take his hand, he laughed. "Okay then. Verbal agreement, it is."

"Agreed."

As I walked out of Wayne's Auto Repair, I felt a sense of pride. I'd done it on my own. The words of the people I'd left behind in New York repeated in my head.

"Let me handle this."

"Just be a good little girl and let the men take care of everything."

"You don't have to do anything but look pretty."

The hell I did. I'd handle whatever came my way. I was an independent woman.

As I walked down the cracked sidewalks of Shady Grove toward the business district, I felt like a lioness. Sure, it was a small feat, negotiating a deal for my car repair, but damn it if I didn't feel like roaring. This was what Katy Perry had been singing about.

I passed the terrible chicken restaurant with the ridiculous name and headed toward a block of small shops, all connected in a row. While the structures of the buildings were all the same aging brick and wood, each storefront had its own personality. An antique store was first, with gingerbread-style trim and a sign that read YESTERYEAR. It was followed by a small hardware store, then a newspaper office, *The Shady Grove Gazette.* I chuckled as I walked past the window and saw two people inside, busily typing away on their computers.

What could they possibly have to report on in this town?

When one of the newspaper workers looked up and caught me staring, she smiled and waved.

Oh shit. What if they're writing about me? What if the out-of-towner is the headline story?

I quickly ducked out of sight and moved on to the next building. The last thing I needed was press, even in a small town. If the story somehow made its way back to New York, someone would surely come and try to find me. To *talk sense into me*, as my father had put it.

I didn't need a talking-to; I needed to be left alone. I needed to do something on my own for once. I'd already imagined the surprise on my parents' faces when they found my apartment empty and my belongings gone. They were probably still pissed that they had to send a church full of people home. Served them right for signing me up for something I didn't agree to.

I took in a deep breath, pleased that the fresh country air seemed to calm my nerves. This place wasn't so bad. With little to no traffic and little to no people, it was a quiet place. A good place to collect yourself. To reflect and plan ahead. Also, a good place to get some much-needed alone time ... or to get my nails done, I realized as I found myself in front of a quaint little salon—Cut and Dyed.

May as well make the most of this morning, I thought as I looked down at my hands and grimaced at my chipped nail polish.

I walked through the door, and the eyes of the three clients and the stylists helping them all focused on me. The clients were all of a certain age, as in old. And the stylists all appeared to be in their mid-forties, each of them modeling the latest in mom cuts.

"Can I help you?" one of the stylists asked from behind the chair of an elderly woman getting perm rods twisted into her hair.

For a moment, I thought I must have entered a time

warp. *Perm rods?*

"I hope so," I said with a smile. "I was hoping to get a manicure." I held up a hand to reveal the remnants of polish on my nails. "And a blowout?"

There was nothing I loved more than someone else doing my hair for me. Back in New York, I went every two or three days. I just hoped to God this place offered more than perms.

"Of course," she said with a smile, and then yelled, "Audrey!" startling not only me, but her client. "Do you have time for a manicure?" she asked a younger-looking girl who stepped into the salon from a back room.

"Sure," Audrey said with a smile.

Unlike her coworkers, Audrey was a little sprite of a thing. Her long dark hair was an unnatural color of burgundy, but it suited her style, which was black jeans and a vintage-looking T-shirt with the words LIVE FREE on the front. Her eyes were dramatically lined with dark charcoal, and tattoos on her arms and collarbone peeked out from her shirt.

"Come on back." She beckoned me with a wave, and the mismatched bangle bracelets on her wrists clinked together in an almost soothing melody. "I'm Audrey, in case you didn't catch that announcement," she said with a chuckle.

I followed her to a small room in the back of the salon, where a nail table was set up in a corner. "I heard."

"Bess is a bit of a loudmouth," she confessed as we took our seats out of earshot of the rest of the crew.

"Saves on an intercom system."

"Sure does." She smiled. "So, you must be the new girl."

"Is that what they're calling me?"

"New girl. Out-of-towner. Broke-down Audi at Wayne's. To name a few," she said with a grin.

"It's Charlotte," I told her.

"Well, Charlotte, it's nice to meet you." She placed a small dish with a self-explanatory decoration in the center that read Rings and Things.

I slipped off the two rings I wore on my right hand and placed them in the dish, then managed to stop myself from reaching for the ring that used to be on my left hand. The phantom weight that I still felt on that fourth finger was starting to fade, but if you looked closely you could see the outline of what used to be. Or, at least, what could have been.

"Do you have a color in mind?" Audrey asked, pulling me back to the present.

"Lincoln Park After Dark," I said without hesitation.

"I like a girl that knows what she wants," she said with a nod. "It's my favorite too." She held up her perfectly manicured hands. "Just touched mine up yesterday."

"It's a staple."

"It really is."

As we bonded over our love of OPI, I had to admit a little pang of jealousy raked through me. Audrey could paint her own nails. *Lucky girl.* Every time I tried to "touch up" my polish, it ended up looking like a drunk toddler had been holding the brush.

I dipped one hand into the bowl of warm, scented water that Audrey offered as she readied her supplies.

"What do you think of Shady Grove?" She picked up my other hand and began to remove the old polish. "Honestly?" she added with a pointed look.

"Well . . ." I hesitated. "It's small."

"Microscopic."

"But it's quaint," I said, trying to be polite.

"It's Podunk."

"Maybe a little. Most of the people are really nice, though."

"They can be." She slipped my polish-free hand back into the water and picked up the other. "Who have you met? Besides Wayne," she said with a chuckle. "He's a trip, right?"

"He is, but he did agree to get my car fixed by Wednesday, so that's good."

"His Wednesday is usually Friday." When a small

sigh slipped from my lips, she added, "But maybe he'll prove me wrong. Enough about him. Who else have you met?"

"Opal at the inn," I said. "She's sweet, and the room she gave me is very nice."

"Great gal."

"And Maggie at Wayne's."

"Nosy gossip," Audrey said matter-of-factly. "Her nickname is Maggie the Mouth."

"Good to know." I laughed.

"Molly Wilder."

"Love her. We actually graduated together."

"She seems awesome," I told her. "And her brothers."

Audrey gave me a sly grin. "Nice to look at, right?"

"They're okay." I shrugged, trying not to fan the fire that seemed to burn inside me when I thought about Luke. They were beyond nice to look at. It was the talking part that I wasn't a fan of. "I haven't had too much interaction with them. Duke seems nice enough, but I know a player when I see one."

"You pegged him." Audrey nodded, confirming my suspicions. "And Luke?"

"Most arrogant man I've ever met."

What was even more frustrating than his arrogance was the fact that no matter how hard I tried, the moment I thought about him, my body heated with more than just anger. My heart rate picked up. My palms became sweaty. My mouth went from dry to wet in seconds as if ready to rip his pants off with my teeth and take care of him from my knees. And I didn't even like the guy. Fucking infuriating was what it was.

"Really?" She began filing my nails. "I'm surprised. He's usually pretty down-to-earth."

"Not to me. So far, my interactions with him have included him telling me that I'm stuck-up and spoiled." Heat rose in my chest as I thought about him. "He's got some nerve, I'll tell you that much. I saw him this morning at the garage, and he actually tried to negotiate with Wayne on my behalf. As if I couldn't do it myself," I scoffed.

"That's terrible," Audrey said. "I hate it when a good-looking man offers his help. What a bastard."

"Right? I don't need a man to take care of me."

"Girl power." Audrey held up a hand in solidarity. "I mean, what kind of asshole would try to help a woman out? Especially in a place that she's never been to, and talking to a mechanic that he's known since birth. One that he probably knows for sure would take advantage of someone that drives a super-expensive car."

I finally realized what Audrey was doing when I noticed the smirk on her face.

"That Luke Wilder is no good, I tell you." She shook her fist toward the ceiling to layer on the sarcasm.

"Shit," I said, realizing that I might have overreacted a bit. "Maybe I was a little harsh on him today."

"Maybe."

"But he did refer to me as a New Yorker with a stick

up my ass, so he's not completely off the hook."

"Well, he's not perfect." She laughed.

"Enough about that," I said, needing to change the subject. If I thought about Luke any longer, I might actually get the urge to go and apologize to his sexy ass. In my defense, I'd spent the last twenty-eight years having men tell me what to do and how to do it. My reaction to Luke was merely a side effect of my current rebellion. "What's an obviously trendy, fashionable chick like you doing here?"

"You know the human intercom out there?" she asked, and I nodded. "That's my mom."

"Hmm. I would have never guessed."

"Yeah, we're night and day, so I went to cosmetology school. Tried to make it in LA for a few months. Ran out of money, and now I'm back," she said, apparently not too thrilled with how things had ended up. "It wasn't exactly what I had planned for my life, but it is what it is. I'm just going to try and make the most of it."

"For what it's worth," I said, watching as she finished trimming back my cuticles. "You give a kick-ass manicure."

"Girl, I know." She grinned. "When we're finished here, I'm going to give you a blowout that will rock your world."

"I can't wait."

Chapter Five

Luke

Monday could kiss my ass. Especially this Monday.

Starting and finishing the day at Wayne's wasn't what I'd planned. First the hose on the truck was crap, and then I had to go back and get a new spark plug for the tractor we used to mow with. On top of that, I'd tried all day not to think about Charlotte. Which was impossible. Sexy little minx kept leaping to the forefront of my mind, giving me the same kind of hell she had that morning. It wasn't my day, that was for damn sure.

When Duke suggested we grab a bucket of beers at the Drunk Skunk—Shady Grove's local watering hole—I'd jumped at the chance to drown my frustrations. Now I was three beers in, and things were starting to look up.

"Here's to giving Wayne way more money than he deserves," Duke said, holding up his beer.

"Seriously." I clinked my bottle against his. "Can we please just have a month where nothing mechanical breaks down?"

"Amen," Duke agreed.

The fact was, we were so damn close to turning a profit at the distillery, we could taste it. With our next batch nearing age, we'd have a new lot to send out to distributors at the end of next month. Hopefully, from there we could finally make Wilder Whiskey a household name.

My brother and I drank our beers, but it didn't take long for him to be distracted by what he called "the local talent."

"You're seriously going to ditch me for the same girls you've been running game on since high school?" I asked when he told me he was going to the back room to play pool with Lacy Danvers.

"First of all, I don't need game," he said. "Look at me."

I shook my head. His arrogance never ceased to amaze me.

"Second, the last time Lacy Danvers was on the roster was junior year. Not sure if you remember, but she got knocked up after high school and married that prick from Hill Crest."

Hill Crest was a rival school a county over. The same school that beat us in the playoffs our senior year. We were still licking our wounds from that loss over a decade later.

"Oh yeah."

"She's divorced now and back with her parents," he explained. "She could be the one that got away, brother."

"I doubt that," I said. Duke hadn't so much as mentioned the girl in ten years. There was no point in arguing the fact that as soon as Duke sealed the deal with Lacy, he'd be on to the next.

That was where he and I differed. He had the attention span of a gnat when it came to women. I, on the other hand, was monogamous to a fault. Sometimes I wished I could be more like Duke with his one-night stands and not giving a shit. I guessed he was more like Mom in that way, able to just shut it off. Hell, he could probably leave Shady Grove just like Mom did and never even glance over his shoulder. Lucky for me, he'd stuck around. After a day like today, I wasn't sure I could handle all this on my own.

"She could be your sister-in-law," Duke said as he slapped a hand on my back.

I laughed. "I'll get the invitations made up."

"Before you do that, why don't you head on over there and take care of that problem we talked about earlier." He nodded in the direction of one very sexy brunette saddled up to the oak bar. "Might turn your Monday around."

I rolled my eyes and shook my head as he walked away. As soon as he was out of sight, I glanced over my shoulder and caught Charlotte's reflection in the mirror that hung behind the bar. Even in the muted lighting, I could see the blue of her eyes. I watched as she took a drink of the clear liquor she had poured over ice, her finger skillfully keeping the lime wedge that floated on top from slipping against her lips.

Man up. You've got nothing to lose.

She already hated me. The way I saw it, the night

would either end with her still hating me—or maybe, just maybe, we'd make peace. My dick perked up in interest. On top of that, I'd come up with a very interesting proposition for her, and I was hoping like hell that I could make her an offer she couldn't refuse.

I stood up from my seat in the back corner and walked over to her. "Figured you for a fruity drink kind of girl."

"Do you know how many calories are in those fruity drinks?" she replied, not looking over. In my peripheral vision, I could see her reflection looking at me.

"You surprised me with the straight vodka."

"How do you know this isn't just water?"

"By the way you pursed your lips when you swallowed, like it burned going down. There are much better things you can put in your mouth."

That got her attention. Those blue eyes snapped to mine and widened as I leaned in a little closer.

"I could help if you're looking for something a little . . . sweeter."

Charlotte didn't nod, but she didn't shake her head either. I took her lack of response as a yes, and wondered for a second exactly what I could get away with.

What if I just went for it and closed the gap between us? What if I pressed my lips against hers and slipped my tongue into that smart little mouth?

As tempting as the notion was, I raised a hand to the bartender instead. "Two glasses of Wilder," I told him. "Neat."

I placed a hand on the back of the empty barstool next to her and waited for her to nod her okay before I sat down.

"Whiskey?" she asked when the glasses were placed in front of us.

"Best whiskey in town."

"You're telling me that this isn't going to burn like the vodka?"

"I'll guarantee it."

"And what makes you so sure?" she said, leaning

over toward me. Her eyes were a little glassy, making me wonder exactly how much of that vodka she'd had to drink.

"Because I made it."

"Sure, you did." She scoffed, clearly not believing me. When I raised my brows to challenge her skepticism, she said, "You're serious?"

"Not a fan of liars. Definitely not one myself."

"Okay then." She picked up her glass and sniffed at the rich amber-colored liquid. "Let's just see." She lifted the glass to her lips and took a small sip.

I did the same, knowing what to expect—the smooth oak finish, the rich vanilla undertones, the sweet aftertaste that made you want to go back for more. As I swallowed mine, I waited anxiously for her reaction.

"Well?"

"Not too bad."

She was cagey, careful not to let me know exactly how much she liked it. But when she took another sip, I knew we had a new fan.

"Can't believe you ever doubted me."

We sat there for a moment, just looking at each other. While she was still wearing the same clothes from this morning, something was different. Her hair was smoother, her makeup a little darker. The pink polish that I'd noticed on her nails had been replaced with an almost black color.

"How was your day?" I asked.

"Great. After dealing with Wayne, I spent the day at the salon."

"You met Audrey?"

"I did." Charlotte gave me a slightly crooked smile. "Don't I look fantastic?"

While I didn't miss her normally biting tones, I could tell she was a little drunk. Especially when she attempted to bat her now fuller lashes at me.

Damn, she's a cute drunk.

"Fantastic. You wanna split a pizza?" I asked, determined to get some food in her before the liquor took over completely.

"Pizza?"

"Yeah, as in pepperoni, cheese, sauce . . . You've had it before, right?" When she answered me with an eye roll, I said, "And don't give me that *too many calories* bullshit."

"Well, it is."

I silenced her with a finger against her pouty lips. "We both need dinner. Humor me. One slice."

I let my finger linger in place for a moment. When her lips puckered slightly against my skin, I had to will my cock into submission. *Not yet, pal.* I dropped my hand from her mouth.

I wasn't the kind of guy who took advantage of a girl who'd had too much to drink. Before I made a move, I'd get some food and water in her. The last thing I wanted was her doing anything she'd regret.

"Fine," she said. "Pizza does sound pretty good."

"That a girl."

• • •

One pizza later, the two of us were sitting at a small table at the front of the bar. While we'd kept our conversation light so far, I couldn't help but think of all the questions I had for Charlotte. My interest in her went far beyond looks.

"I learned a little bit about you today," she said.

"Don't believe everything you hear." I was pretty sure my reputation in this town was golden, but you never know what's said behind closed doors.

"All good, I promise."

"What did you hear?"

"You've got a lot of fans," she said with a smile. "Of the female variety."

"I don't know about that."

I tried to keep to myself and ignore a lot of the attention younger women throw my way. But I could have gone on for days about how doing the right thing hadn't always panned out the way I'd hoped. Didn't keep my mom around. Or Sarah.

I decided against opening up, though. I barely knew this girl, and the last thing I wanted was to bare my soul to a sexy stranger passing through. A subject change was needed.

"So . . . how exactly did you end up here?"

"Long story," she said with a sigh.

"I've got no place to be."

"Well . . ."

I could see her hesitation in revealing her reasons, which only made me want to know more.

"I'm on my way to LA," she finally said. "I'm moving in with a friend."

"Boyfriend? Girlfriend?"

"A girl that's a friend. Valentina."

"Okay." I could hear the relief in my own voice. "New York girl moves to LA. That's a big move. You running from something?"

"The law," she said plainly, causing me to nearly choke on the water I'd just drank.

"Seriously?"

Her lips twitched. "I shot a man in Reno."

When I realized she was yanking my chain, I was relieved and more than a little turned on by the girl's wit. New Yorkers were pegged as being street smart, but this one didn't miss a beat, so I played along.

"Just to watch him die?"

"You know my story?" She chuckled, and I laughed along with her.

"I'm familiar. Johnny Cash is a favorite around here. I'm surprised you know who he is."

She grinned. "Even New York isn't immune to a little country charm."

That's what I was hoping. She wanted country charm, and I had it in spades. Hell, truckloads. I'd turn it up and get exactly what I wanted from her.

"I just need a fresh start," she said, confessing as much as I thought I was going to get out of her that night.

Whatever she was leaving behind in New York

wasn't something she was ready to talk about, which was fine by me. When I'd walked over here, I was aiming for simple and easy. Too much talk of the past might lead someplace I didn't think either of us were looking to end up.

"Fresh starts are good. I've needed a couple in my life." The urge to clear up the bad blood between us was weighing on me. Seemed like as good a time as any. "Maybe we get one? I might not have made the best first impression."

"Me either," she admitted. "I was a jerk too. I promise I'm not a complete asshole."

"Same here. All is forgiven."

The truth was, seeing her sitting there with her kissable lips and a look of vulnerability that I hadn't seen from her yet, I would have pardoned her for actually shooting a man in Reno.

"To fresh starts," she said, raising her glass of water.

"To fresh starts." I nodded and clinked my glass against hers, grinning back at her. "So, about what you mentioned yesterday, a marketing degree from Yale."

"What about it?"

"Any chance I could convince you to use it to help me out?"

The cutest little line formed between her brows as she processed what I was saying.

"See, I've got this fantastic whiskey that needs selling, and I'm about as useless as tits on a nun when it comes to social media and all that shit."

She giggled. "Are you asking me to help you market your whiskey, Luke?"

"Yes."

"What's in it for me?"

"What do you want?" I teased, letting our stare linger for a few seconds. I would have given my left arm for her to say something along the lines of *I want you to fuck my brains out*. Especially when she ran the tip of her tongue over her lips as she thought.

"What do you have to offer?" she said, shifting a little in her seat.

As much as she was getting to me, I could see that she was feeling it too. The sexual tension. The heat. The chemistry. It was undeniable.

"I can think of a few things." I rested my forearms on the table and leaned closer. The sweet smell of her expensive perfume was intoxicating.

"Well . . ." She leaned forward, mirroring my position, and it took a lot of willpower not to toss the table between us across the room. "I can think of one thing," she said softly, drawing me in even more. "I'd really like that car part you said your buddy could ship from Austin."

"You got it," I mustered up, drowning out the lust that was about to rip me in two. Never in my life had a woman riled me up the way this one did. My dick was so hard, I could have used it to pound nails, and all we'd done was sit here and talk tonight.

"Good," she said with a huge grin. "You've got a deal."

Chapter Six

Charlotte

Two hours later, Luke and I stood in the parking lot of the bar. I leaned against the side of his big black truck as I watched him, my lips turned up in a smile.

"Turns out you're not so bad," he said, his mouth twitching as he watched me.

"That so?" I placed a hand on my hip.

Leaning closer, he tucked a stray lock of hair behind my ear and shrugged. "When you're not running your mouth, you can be downright tolerable."

When his full lips blossomed into a wide smile, something inside me zinged. Laughing, I shook my head.

We'd spent the evening talking, eating pizza, and sipping on whiskey. I felt relaxed and loose. All my worries had taken a back seat to this gorgeous man with his cocky personality and mega-white smile.

Luke couldn't seem to stop touching me—his hand at my lower back as he led me from the bar, the way he rose to his feet and helped me from my bar stool when I needed to use the restroom, and now, his fingertips grazing my bare arms and then touching my hair. His attention was dizzying, because I wasn't used to forward men.

Well, that wasn't true. I was used to men who were forward with their self-accolades. Bragging about how much money they'd made in the stock market, about their Fifth Avenue address or their job title. Those were things I was used to.

Luke was the complete opposite. I wasn't used to a man who had nothing to offer but himself and yet gave it so freely—letting his interest be known, to hell with the consequences. Because the two of us? We made absolutely no sense. I would be leaving soon, and I had a feeling he would live out his life here and die in the same place he'd been born.

We couldn't be more different, but our bodies didn't care. The chemistry zipping between us fueled an attraction that grew with every barb we lobbed at each other. He was fun and challenging in a way that was entirely new.

"When you feed me whiskey all night, what did you

expect? I tend to lose my filter," I said, lifting my chin.

"I did feed you more than whiskey. I wasn't a complete asshole tonight."

I nodded, remembering the pizza we'd shared. "For once."

His mouth twitched again. "I kinda like you when you're full of whiskey, duchess."

That damn nickname again.

He winked at me, and I almost melted into a puddle right there in the dusty gravel parking lot. For the longest time, we stayed like that—our eyes locked together, our hips lined up, his hand at my waist . . .

Are you gonna kiss me, or what?

I didn't have to wonder any longer. Luke's gaze darkened and he lowered his head toward mine. I lifted onto my toes, needing to close the distance between us fast. He took my mouth with a soft kiss and I immediately responded, parting my lips. His tongue moved against mine in deep, drugging kisses that made my toes curl in my sneakers.

Damn, the man could kiss.

Turned out his truck wasn't his only big possession. To my whiskey-soaked brain, it felt like a massive steel rod was tucked inside his jeans. Jesus, he was hung.

Come to Mama.

An older man headed to his car whistled at us. "Looks like somebody's gettin' lucky tonight."

Luke cursed under his breath and grabbed my hand. "People in this town are fuckin' nosy. Come on."

Inside the cab of his truck, the scent of oil, leather, and whiskey created a warm, cozy atmosphere.

"Where are we going?" I asked.

"I'm driving you back to the inn."

Disappointment flashed through me. *Damn.* So, we weren't going back to his place for wild sex.

"How do you know that's where I'm staying?"

His answer was a smirk on those gorgeous full lips. "God, you're cute when you're sassy. It's the only hotel in town."

When we pulled to a stop in the parking lot of the little Victorian house that had been converted to a bed and breakfast, Luke shifted the truck into park and cut the engine.

"You want to come inside?" My voice trembled only slightly, but my heart was jack-hammering against my ribs.

"Better not." His voice was rough, and I sensed his restraint was hanging by a thread, just like mine. "People in this town talk." He reached over and placed his hand on my knee, giving it a squeeze. "Plus, I'm not gonna lie. I'm attracted to you, duchess, and I might not behave like a gentleman if I come inside."

"Maybe I'm done with guys who pretend to be perfect gentlemen."

He released a growl of frustration and leaned in closer, placing a soft kiss on my jaw. He could be such a stubborn, rough-around-the edges prick, and then other times, he could be so sweet and tender.

"I almost hate to admit this," I said, "but I had fun with you tonight."

"Me too," he murmured with his lips inches from mine.

Wetting my lips with my tongue, I fought off a smile at the way his hungry gaze tracked the movement. He started slow, his lips hovering at my jaw before he peppered soft kisses against my neck.

"Luke," I groaned. I wanted this, and I had no idea what had come over me. Maybe it was part of being on the run, but I wanted to sin. Wanted him to make me forget everything—my past, my mistakes . . . hell, even my own damn name.

Capturing my mouth in a hungry kiss, he lashed his tongue at mine and I took everything he offered. The feel of his rough, calloused fingertips grazing my skin, the taste of whiskey on his breath, his masculine scent—it was intoxicating.

Climbing over the center console, I planted myself in his lap and pushed my hands into his hair as I kissed him back. His kisses were rough and intense, and I couldn't help but wonder about the way this man fucked. Would he take me hard and fast, or draw things out until I was a whimpering mess?

Moving in his lap until I found the right angle, I pushed my hips closer, grinding against the steely erection behind his zipper that pressed at my core.

His deep groan of frustrated need made my inner muscles clench.

As I worked myself against him, we continued kissing, his hands locked on my hips as I rolled them against his. All my cards were on the table. I wanted him and he knew it. And lucky for me, it seemed he wanted me just as badly.

Luke gripped my ass, working me against his cock. I was close, so close. Just a little more pressure . . .

"Time out." He groaned.

Time out? Did he just call a timeout? Putting a few inches of space between us, I blinked to clear my hazy vision and gazed up at him.

"I'm not fucking you in my truck. And if we go any further, that's what's going to happen."

My heart pounding, my panties soaked, I crawled from his lap. Partly annoyed at him and partly annoyed at myself for getting carried away, I grabbed my purse and opened the door.

Outside the truck, the fresh air did wonders to clear my head. I was never like this.

Luke's sly smile was back as he hopped out of the truck, and he was back to rubbing my arms. "What are you doing tomorrow?"

Wasn't that a good question? "I don't know. I'll have to check my schedule," I snapped, still mad at him for calling a damn timeout.

He chuckled again, low under his breath, and the sound vibrated against my skin. I had no idea how it was possible for this man to get under my skin so deeply, so quickly, but he had.

"I was thinking if you're free, I'd show you around the distillery. But you know, only if you're free."

The wiseass. He knew I had nothing to do but sit around and wait for my car to get fixed.

"I'm free," I huffed.

"I'll pick you up at eight."

My eyebrows shot up. "In the morning?"

"Okay, make it ten," he said with a chuckle. "And be ready to put that marketing genius to work."

"You got it."

• • •

At five to ten when Luke showed up the next morning, I was up, showered, and dressed. My hair was still damp, but when I saw him standing there at the foot of the stairs, holding two paper cups of hot coffee, the last thing I wanted was to spend twenty minutes blow-drying my hair and putting on makeup when Luke probably didn't care about things like that anyway.

Besides, that was the old Charlotte, always put together and polished. And look where it had gotten me. Nowhere.

"Ready?" he asked, looking up at me from the parlor where Opal had left him.

I winked. "Give me thirty seconds."

In the adjoining bathroom, I pulled my still-damp

hair into a high messy ponytail and dabbed on some lip balm. *There.* I was ready.

My cell phone chimed, and I glanced down at it with a scowl. My parents. Again. Hitting a button to silence it, I stuffed it in the back pocket of my jeans. I wasn't ready to face them or all the shit I left behind when I hightailed it out of New York.

"That was fast," Luke said as he handed me a cup of coffee.

The surprise in his tone told me that was unexpected. I decided that I liked this new Charlotte, liked doing the opposite of what people expected.

"Cream and sugar in yours. Hope that's all right."

"It's perfect." I took a sip of the warm brew.

"How are you feeling this morning?" Luke asked as we climbed into his truck.

I wasn't sure if he was referring to the whiskey we'd downed last night, or the way he'd left me riled up and aroused.

"I slept like a baby." At least, that much was true. I

was still slightly annoyed at him for the way he'd called things off last night, but I'd never admit that to him.

A few minutes later, we turned off the main road and onto his property, rolling hills and grassy pastures dotted with massive pecan trees.

"This is me." He pointed to a pale brick two-story house at the top of the hill. A former farmhouse, it had a wide front porch and plantation-style shutters painted a glossy black framing the windows.

"All of that just for you?"

He shook his head. "Duke and Molly and I all live there. Dad left it to us."

My throat suddenly felt dry, and I took another sip of coffee. I recalled what Opal had said about Luke's past.

After parking his truck beside the quintessential red barn at the far end of his property, we climbed into something Luke called a side-by-side, which to me looked like a revved-up golf cart.

We cruised around the acreage while Luke pointed things out to me—the tree house he and his brother built when they were twelve, the pond where he got caught skinny-dipping with the pastor's daughter. It was crazy how comfortable Luke and I were together. I'd known him a mere forty-eight hours, and yet we felt like old friends.

The fresh country air and sunshine did wonders for my mood. I was happy that I'd opted not to style my hair. Hell, I was just plain happy.

"Careful now, duchess. If you smile any harder, I might go and think you're actually enjoying yourself."

The playful edge to his voice was addictive. After only a short couple of days, I could already feel myself falling for his charms.

A little while later, we finally stopped in front of the distillery and climbed out, stretching our legs.

"You wanna see where the magic happens?" Luke asked.

I rolled my eyes, following him toward the building that was rustic, but cute. "Why do I feel like that's a cheesy pickup line you've used a thousand times to seduce a thousand girls?"

He halted in his tracks and turned to face me. "There are two things you need to know. First, this isn't some ploy to get you into bed. I was serious about wanting your help."

I nodded. "And the second?"

"There haven't been a thousand women." And then he smiled. "Maybe only nine hundred or so."

The tinge of something darker in his gaze told me he had a story in his past that he used humor to hide, maybe something just as deep and painful as my own. But I didn't want to think about all that just now, so I grinned back at him and followed him inside.

It took a moment for my eyes to adjust to the dim lighting. It was warm and reminded me of a bread factory—humid and with a yeasty smell hanging in the air. Big wooden vats and huge copper canisters bubbled with the fermented sugars from rye and corn.

Luke pointed things out to me as we made our way through. I didn't know anything about whiskey or bourbon, but it was cool to hear him talk about something he was passionate about. And he was clearly passionate about whiskey, or maybe he was just emotional about his family business. When he spoke about the aging and bottling process, he became animated, using his hands to talk, and watched me with a smile to make sure I was keeping up.

"This place is great, Luke. I can see why you're so proud of it."

"Glad you approve, duchess."

After passing through an aging room filled with oak barrels, Luke led me to what he called his tasting room. Chocolate-brown velvet armchairs and a rustic wooden table sat in the center of the room. A bottle of whiskey with a tray of rocks glasses was waiting for us. The room was tastefully decorated in rich, masculine colors. A black-and-white photograph of a Texas longhorn hung on one wall, and the other wall was filled with windows overlooking the pastures.

"Care for a taste?" Luke motioned for me to sit as he picked up the bottle.

I'd only just finished my coffee, and now we were going to drink whiskey? "Maybe just a sip. It's early."

He nodded and poured a splash into each of our glasses.

I sniffed at the liquor, watching him over the rim of my glass. I'd had Wilder whiskey last night, but that was after several cocktails. "What should I be looking for? Any tips?"

He lifted his glass, inspecting it. "Deep golden color. Intense aroma. Hints of smoky caramel with a sweet maple finish." He downed the contents in one swallow, his full lips hovering seductively on the rim of the glass. "The charred oak barrels are used only once. Each one is a tiny bit unique, and they flavor the final product."

I took a swallow, then licked my lips. "Smooth."

He nodded. "It's good for sipping."

Setting my glass down, I turned to face Luke, my interest in this place piqued. "Do you offer tastings here?"

He shook his head. "We're not open to the public."

"You should really consider it, play up the local angle. You need to advertise that each bottle was handmade right here. People eat that stuff up."

He opened his mouth like he wanted to argue some point with me, then thought better of it.

"Thought I heard voices." Duke strolled into the tasting room and joined us. "Breaking your own rules, I see," he said to Luke.

"Little brother." Luke tipped his head toward Duke. "You need something?"

Duke shook his head and then reached for my hand, lifting it to his mouth for a quick kiss. "Shame to see you get mixed up with the riffraff."

"I'll be careful. I promise."

Duke tugged his ball cap lower over his eyes and shot me a soul-filled look as he turned away. "I've got work to do. You two be good," he called over his shoulder.

Once he was gone, I took another sip of my whiskey, watching Luke over the rim of my glass. "What did he mean about breaking your rules?"

He was quiet for a moment, and I thought he wasn't going to tell me. It would have served me right because of the monumental secret I was keeping from him. A secret that was starting to knaw at me.

"We made a pact a long time ago. The tasting room is 'no girls allowed.'"

"Oh." I shifted in my seat, wondering why that rule was instituted and what it meant that I was sitting here.

"It was started to keep Molly out, but then it just became more. Like this was our place—a spot for Duke and me to talk business, and to get away from everything else."

I nodded. I understood that. Growing up the way I did, I cherished my down time. It wasn't uncommon for me to sneak out of an important family function at my father's country club to go hang out in the kitchen or the coat room with the staff. They were always way more fun. It was often the only chance I got to let my hair down and relax.

"I don't mean to pry, but you said something earlier about your dad leaving you this place." Reading between the lines, I was assuming he meant his dad had passed.

"There's not much to tell. After my mom took off,

he had nothing left to live for and drank himself to an early death."

I blinked, surprised by Luke's brutal honesty. "I'm sorry."

"Don't be." He shrugged. "It was a long time ago."

"So, your mom is . . ."

"She left when I was seven, but to be honest, she was gone a long time before that, emotionally. It was no secret that she hated it here. When she couldn't take it anymore, she took off for city life. Got remarried and had a whole other family, last I heard."

I swallowed. That would have been tough for a little kid to handle. No wonder Luke was so hardened. His steely exterior was in place for a reason—most likely a defense mechanism so he couldn't get too close to someone who might abandon him ever again.

"Well, for what it's worth, thanks for bringing me here today."

"I'm glad you got to see it. Do you think you can help?"

"I know I can."

My mind was already buzzing with ideas. Opening to the public to offer tastings and food pairings and seasonal gifts was only the beginning. I could envision events like weddings and banquets under the gazebo by the pond. The excitement of building a brand like this from scratch was intoxicating.

Luke rose to his feet. "I've got some e-mails to catch up on and a conference call with a distributor, but maybe we can talk about your ideas later?"

"Absolutely. I just need a quiet place to work, and a pen and a pad. I'm going to draft up an entire marketing strategy for you."

Luke's eyes widened slightly. "If it's too much trouble or too much to ask, I understand—"

I raised a hand, cutting him off. "Honestly, what else am I going to do? Sit around and stare at the phone, waiting for Wayne to call?"

"Fair enough. Come on. I'll set you up at my favorite spot to brainstorm."

I followed him back to the side-by-side. When we reached his house, Luke led me up the front steps of his wide front porch and stretched out his arms.

"This suit you okay?"

There were wooden armchairs with fluffy cream-colored cushions, and a potted fern on the outdoor coffee table.

"This is perfect."

"Let me get you that pen and paper."

Luke headed inside while I lowered myself into a chair to wait for him. When he returned, he handed me a pad of paper, a couple of pens, a glass of iced tea, and a blueberry muffin.

"Molly made those this morning."

"Thanks. I should be all set."

"I'll check on you in a couple of hours. If you need something or want me to take you back to the inn, just text me."

"I'll be fine."

Sitting inside the little hotel room at the inn held no appeal. I didn't want to admit it to Luke, but I loved the thought of working here instead of a stuffy office. I could see myself doing some good work here. Making a real difference in their business.

The sweet, fresh air fragranced with lilacs and the warm breeze on my skin were a welcome treat. We didn't have quiet, relaxing places like this back home. Although I'd missed all the conveniences of the city over the past few days, in this moment, there was no place I'd rather be.

The realization was like a freight train roaring through my chest. At first, all I'd wanted was to flee this small town, and now I suddenly found myself hoping for a few more days here.

• • •

A few hours later, I shifted in my seat. My stomach reminded me that I'd worked through lunch, and my bladder piped up to remind me of the iced tea I'd downed hours ago.

Rising to my feet, I stretched and contemplated what to do. Text Luke? Ask him to take me home? Sneaking inside to find a bathroom won out.

"Luke?" I opened the front door and let myself inside.

An oak staircase off the foyer was about all I could see. I continued past it toward what I assumed was the kitchen and called his name again.

"Hey. In here."

I turned and saw Luke standing in the doorway of his office, a room off the dining room that held a large oak desk and several tall bookcases.

"I'm sorry to barge in, but can I use your bathroom?"

"Of course. Down the hall on the right."

I hurried past him, and once I'd done my business, I found him on the porch, flipping through the notebook I'd left on the coffee table.

"Hey, give me that. No peeking."

I grabbed it from him, a little self-conscious about my messy chicken scratch and random notes. He handed over the notepad without a fight, but stepped closer until we were standing just inches apart.

Luke had been so open today, sharing a piece of his past with me and letting me into his life. It was unexpected. And working up a marketing plan all day meant I didn't have time to dwell on my own issues—for which I was incredibly grateful.

As he gazed down at me, his eyes went soft. I wet my lower lip, sure he was about to kiss me, but the sound of a car driving up made me step back.

"Hey!" Molly climbed out of her car and reached for a grocery bag. "Fancy seeing you here!"

Chapter Seven

Luke

My sister's timing sucked. Had for years. The brat had the audacity to be born during our Little League championship game, abruptly stealing my thunder when I hit my first home run.

Keeping up her perfect record, Molly had just interrupted a kiss that I'd been working for—and thinking about—all afternoon. And now she had the nerve to beam at us as she joined us on the porch.

"Stay for dinner," Molly insisted when Charlotte said she'd better get going.

I nodded when Charlotte looked in my direction, gauging my reaction. If she stayed, I might get another chance at that kiss.

"I'm grilling fish," Molly told her, and added with a wink, "Healthy."

Charlotte smiled. "I really have no choice then, do I."

"No, ma'am." Molly pulled open the screen door, glowing in her triumph. "It will be ready in fifteen."

"She must have been planning this," I told Charlotte in a low voice once we were alone again. "She said earlier we were eating spaghetti tonight."

"It's sweet."

"That's Molly. Sweet." I shook my head. "Not at all manipulative."

Charlotte laughed. "That's a strong word."

It wasn't the first time that day she'd let out that laugh, so easy and natural. If I didn't know any better, I'd think she actually liked this place, and my family. Me, even. After the way things got heated last night, I wasn't sure if we'd be able to get back to friendly, but here we were.

"She's just trying to be welcoming," Charlotte said.

"Mm-hmm."

Knowing Molly's game, I was skeptical. Get Charlotte to stay, and maybe her brother's mood would improve. As much as my sister's tricks usually annoyed me, I was happy that Charlotte had agreed to stay.

Charlotte glanced away. "I can go if you don't want me to stay."

"No, no . . . it's not that. I . . ." I stammered through my sentence like a teenage boy before I remembered that I was a grown-ass man, a man who knew what he wanted. Charlotte was looking me in the eye, waiting for something intelligible to come out of my mouth, and I needed to man up. "I want you to stay."

For dinner. For the night. Maybe longer.

But I wouldn't say that. Not out loud. She was only here for a short time, and I had to get my head wrapped around that. I hadn't expected the way she'd dived in today, asking questions about my business and wanting to help craft a marketing strategy. It sounded awful now that I knew Charlotte, but when I first saw her, I'd assumed she was the kind of girl who was allergic to hard work. She just kept surprising me.

"You sure?"

"Positive."

"Good."

• • •

By the time Charlotte and I were seated at the table on the patio, the sun was setting. It was my favorite time of day. Seeing the wide-open Texas sky painted in orange and pink always had a calming effect on me.

Duke came in from whatever it was that he did all day. I'd learned to stop asking a long time ago. As long as he showed up when and where I needed his help, I couldn't have given a rat's ass about what—or who—he was doing.

"Charlotte, how nice of you to grace us with your presence," he teased as he joined us. "Not every day we get to dine with a sophisticated New Yorker."

"I consider it charity work," she said with a smirk as he sat down across from her. "Small-town outreach program, helping to get the delinquents back on the right path." She tilted her head as she joked with him. The few remaining rays of sunlight caught her hair and made it glow, giving her an angelic appearance.

"You're a real ballbuster, you know that," Duke said with a chuckle. "I like it."

So did I. Besides the fact that Charlotte was insanely gorgeous, she was incredibly smart and witty. I'd never met a woman like her. The girls I'd dated before were just that . . . girls. Charlotte was a woman. Polished, educated, well spoken. She knew how to stand her ground, which might just be the sexiest thing about her.

"So, smarty-pants," Duke said to her. "You come up with a marketing plan for the distillery yet?"

She nodded. "Working on it. I'm thinking we sell the lifestyle as opposed to just the whiskey."

"And in terms a delinquent like me could understand?" Duke asked.

"Small-town, simple, laid back," she said. "I think people would eat it up. Especially city people. You don't know how many times I've heard someone from New York say they wished they could just leave it all behind."

It occurred to me to ask if that's what she was doing, but I tamped down the notion. Getting any more invested in her situation—her running away from New York—was the last thing I needed to do. This was a business arrangement. The possibility of getting a little more from her was a bonus. Anything that happened physically between us needed to be just that. Lines needed to be drawn in the sand, both for my sake and hers. *Keep it simple, stupid.*

"I love it," Molly chimed in as she brought the food to the table. "We love this place. Everyone else should too."

"I agree," Charlotte said.

"You think people are really interested in a place like Shady Grove?" I asked. "I mean, I think it's great, but it's not like they're clamoring to come visit."

"They will be," Charlotte said with confidence. "I think the first thing we need to do, besides get all of your social media accounts up to par, is set up an event. Sort of an official launch of the brand."

Duke grinned. "I love parties."

I kicked him under the table, keeping my focus on Charlotte. "And where exactly were you thinking?"

"Here," she said matter-of-factly.

"I don't know about that—"

"It's perfect," she said. "People need to see this place, need to see the distillery. They need to meet the family behind the whiskey."

The mere thought of it made me itch, and I scowled at her. "I don't want a bunch of strangers traipsing around the property. We live here, you know. It's not a goddamn roadside attraction."

"Luke." Molly glared at me. "You want to sell all those barrels, right?"

"Yeah, man," Duke said, adding to the current pileup on me. "You wanted a marketing guru. Now you need to listen to her."

"I don't know . . ." It didn't set well with me, but they were right. I had asked Charlotte to come up with ideas to help us make money. If this was her plan, I needed to hear it out. "I guess we could give it a try."

My brother and sister grinned at each other as Charlotte leaned over and placed a kiss on my cheek. The pleased look on her face was enough to knock down my resolve a little, and the unexpected feel of her lips on my skin blasted the rest of the way through.

I was fucked with a capital *F*.

Chapter Eight

Charlotte

"Mornin', this is Maggie. Can I help you?" the voice drawled through the phone.

"Hi, this is Charlotte Freemont. I'm calling about—"

"The Audi. Yup. Let me put Wayne on."

Sitting down on the bed, I plucked a piece of lint off the fluffy down comforter while I waited.

"This is Wayne." His normally gruff voice came out sounding apologetic. "Listen, sweetheart, I hate to tell you this, but I ran your car's diagnostics through the computer, and you've got a bigger problem than I first thought."

I listened as he explained that some converter switch was malfunctioning, and that it was going to add an extra day or two and some money to the repair work.

"Okay, got it."

"That's . . . that's it?" he asked.

"Yeah. Just let me know when you're through. I

appreciate this, Wayne."

"Of course, sweetheart. I'll be in touch."

I should have been annoyed, should have felt trapped and isolated, but I felt anything but. It was crazy, but part of me was excited at the idea of spending a few more days here.

I dialed Valentina next, who answered without even a hello.

"Charlotte, tell me you're on your way. I'm freaking out."

"Hello to you too." I chuckled.

"Ugh, what's happening? You're not still stranded, are you?"

"I'm still here, yeah."

"Whose ass do I need to kick? I'll call the mechanic myself. Just tell me where you are."

"No, it's fine, Val." It was weird, but the desire to keep this place a secret flared inside me. It was like if I could shield it from the outside world, I could stay here in peace for a few more days.

She let out a huff of frustration and cursed in Spanish.

We spent the next few minutes catching up on everything going on back home, in the real world, and it was weird. Normally, I'd eat up this kind of conversation. Gossiping with Valentina was practically an Olympic sport, one I excelled at, but today I was only half listening.

"Just a couple more days. I'll see you soon," I said, finally ending the call.

As soon as we hung up, my phone rang again. It was Molly.

"Hi, Charlotte. I was wondering if you'd want to have lunch with me today?"

My gaze drifted to the clock beside my bed. I had all day to kill. "Sure. What time?"

"I'll meet you at the Garden of Eatin' in thirty minutes."

I picked up my purse and slipped into my nude Tori Butch flats before heading downstairs to ask Opal how to get to the restaurant. It turned out it was only three blocks away, so I'd get in a little midday sunshine and a brief walk. My time here was starting to feel more like a vacation than a death sentence.

The café was cozy chic with rustic little white-painted tables and mismatched chairs. It had character, and the menu was just as eclectic. Everything from chicken and waffles to grits (whatever those were) to spinach salad with fresh goat cheese. Maggie and I were soon seated at a table in front of the big front windows, each having found something on the menu to our liking.

"Thanks for meeting me." Molly tasted her iced tea, then tore open a packet of sweetener and dumped it in.

"Of course. Not like I had anything better to do. Wayne thinks it'll be another couple of days." When her mouth puckered at that, I shook my head. "I'm sorry, that came out wrong. Everyone's been so welcoming since I've been here."

"Luke has been more 'welcoming' than I've seen him with a newcomer in a long time."

I thought Molly might give me a saucy wink or a

smile with that comment, but her expression remained serious. She tasted her iced tea again and found it more to her liking before she continued.

"Listen, I think it's great you're interested in my brother, but I think there are a few things you should know."

Ah. The real reason she asked me to lunch. "Okay."

"Luke acts tough, and he is, but he's been hurt before. He's been through a lot; we all have. I just don't want to see him get left behind again."

I got the sense that she wasn't talking about their mother's leaving town. My mind churned with possibilities, and my curiosity was too strong to try to be polite.

Screw that. If anyone would know, Molly would, so if I had to pump her for information, I would.

"Has he been in a serious relationship before?" I asked point-blank.

Molly focused on her salad like it was the most interesting thing she'd seen all day. "He has. But that's not my place to tell." She then looked up and smiled at me as she turned the conversation to safer ground.

I was dying to push, but smiled back and let her have her way. Our conversation left me with more questions than answers.

Chapter Nine

Luke

If I didn't know any better, I would say that Charlotte Freemont was really starting to like Shady Grove. The moment she came bouncing through the door of the bar with my sister, her face lit up when she saw the crowd. It was Thursday night and the Drunk Skunk was packed—packed with wandering eyes that followed Charlotte's every move as she walked my way.

I got it, though. She was gorgeous and had an aura of mystery surrounding her that drew the attention of every hot-blooded man in the room. I hated every one of those motherfuckers looking at her.

Eyes off my girl.

My girl? There was a thought I didn't have every day. Last time I'd wanted a girl to be mine, I'd ended up getting my heart torn to shreds. I needed to be careful when it came to Charlotte. I barely knew her, but somehow my subconscious was staking claim. And I'd had just enough to drink to roll with it.

"Evening, duchess," I said, sliding an arm around her

waist when she was close enough. A subtle vibration jolted through her as our bodies pressed against each other. She melded against me like it was right where she belonged.

"Hello there." She looked up at me, her big blue eyes crystal clear and sparkling with excitement. "How was your day?"

"Better now. Yours?"

"Same," she said, biting at her bottom lip.

The crowd around us seemed to fade away, leaving just the two of us. It had been a few days since our last kiss, and I hadn't been able to stop thinking about it. The way she'd tasted. The soft moans she let out. The way her body reacted under my touch. Even when we were talking business, the thoughts of ravaging her were always there.

Tonight was the night it was going to happen, come hell or high water.

"You look good enough to eat," I said, loving the way her hair was loosely curled and her makeup was just enough to accentuate every beautiful feature of her face.

The upper curves of her fantastically perfect tits were peeking out from her V-necked shirt. Taking a bite of her was going to be fun. I wet my lips as I ran a hand over her waist.

"I thought you two hated each other," Duke said with a grin, drawing our attention.

"Things change." I glared at him, needing my brother's comments like I needed a hole in the head.

"Yeah, I think I kind of like him now." Charlotte rested her head against my chest and gave Duke a shrug.

"Give it a few days. It'll wear off," Duke told her, earning a slap on the shoulder from me.

"Thanks, buddy." I turned my attention back to Charlotte. "You want to eat? Dance? Have a drink?" I ran through the list of options for the night, hoping the lust-filled look in her eyes meant she was thinking the same thing I was, which was none of the above.

"Maybe you two need to just get a room," Molly suggested, breaking the trance that linked the two of us.

"I tried." Charlotte chuckled. "Your brother is too

much of a gentleman."

"I don't have to be," I whispered in her ear with a growl.

Her body tensed, and I could practically hear the excited thump of her heart. We'd tiptoed around this sexual tension for long enough. Just because I'd ended our first night by not jumping into bed with her didn't mean I was going to do the same thing now. My cock had been begging for days, and I was ready to do something about it.

"Want to get out of here?" I asked.

She gave me a subtle nod and a smile as I laced my fingers through hers. The feel of her petite hand in mine was a natural fit, which added fuel to the fire already building inside me.

"As much fun as this place is, we've got to go," I told Duke and Molly.

"Have fun, you two," Duke shouted over the music as I led Charlotte through the crowd toward the exit.

As soon as we were outside, I pulled her into my

arms and gave her the proper greeting that she deserved. My lips found hers in an instant. My tongue greedily slipped into her mouth as I held her close. Once I knew I'd left her breathless, I resumed the hand-holding and led her to my truck.

"What's gotten into you?" she asked with a laugh as I opened the passenger door for her.

"Decided I was done wasting time, duchess," I replied with a smirk. "Too much? Too fast?"

"No, I like it." She pressed her body against mine as she lifted one foot onto the running board and stood on the tiptoes of the other. "A man who knows what he wants is always sexy," she added as she pressed her lips softly against my cheek.

The angle of her body gave me the perfect opportunity to show her exactly what I wanted. Looping an arm around her waist, I pressed the steel of my cock against her center. She moaned at the contact as I put my lips on hers. I could feel the heat radiating from her and nearly came on the spot.

I'd been thinking all day about where I wanted to

take Charlotte tonight. I broke our kiss and carefully shut her inside the truck. One more second of her temptation, and our first time was going to be in the parking lot of the Drunk Skunk.

"Where are you taking me?" she asked when I situated myself behind the wheel and started the engine.

"Anywhere you want to go."

I took her hand and drew it to my mouth, pressing my lips against the back of it as my eyes found hers. Dark curls framed her face, and her lips parted as she took in a soft breath. My libido was in overdrive, seriously blurring the reality of what was happening between us.

"To the moon then," she said with a grin.

"You got it." I pulled out of the parking lot and headed to the most romantic spot I knew.

• • •

"Is this place for real?" she asked when we arrived at our destination. The moon looked close enough to touch as it gleamed full and bright in the inky sky.

Charlotte quickly hopped out of the truck to take in our surroundings. A gentle breeze picked up, stirring the tops of the trees that ringed the open field. There were places out in the middle of nowhere that were like heaven on earth, and this was one of them.

"It's real."

I walked up behind her and wrapped my arms around her waist. The grassy hilltop we were standing on was at the far edge of our property, a place I was always drawn to when I needed some alone time. And alone time was exactly what I wanted right now with Charlotte. No interruptions. Just peace and quiet—and her.

"See that speck of light over there," I said, pointing across the way. "That's the house. And over there . . ." I pointed out a ribbon of lights in the opposite direction. "That's Shady Grove."

"This is beautiful." She settled into my arms with a sigh. "It's so peaceful."

"It's a good place to think. I love it out here." As I spoke, tall grasses swayed, stirred by the breeze, and millions of stars shimmered overhead. It truly was magical here.

"Me too." She looked over her shoulder at me. "Thank you for bringing me."

"I may have had some ulterior motives." I dropped a quick kiss on her lips before heading to the truck for the blanket I'd thrown in earlier. I returned to her side and spread it out on the grass. "This is a good spot for more than just thinking."

"A picnic?" she teased.

"Yep." I crouched to take a seat and tugged her by the hand into my lap. "Guess who's on the menu?"

I didn't give her time to respond. Instead, I captured her mouth with mine and let my kiss answer the question for her.

Our make-out session turned into more when Charlotte climbed off my lap and lay on the blanket, tugging me by the shirt on top of her. The horizontal position we found ourselves in was giving me all kinds of ideas, especially when she spread her legs and let me slip my hips between them. She lifted slightly, digging her heels into the ground, increasing the friction between us.

Every time I moved against her, she let out ragged little whimpers.

"You trying to kill me?" I said, feeling like I was about to burst at the seams.

"Not yet. There's something I'd like first." She reached between us and palmed the bulge between my legs. Her slender fingers gripped me through the denim, and damn, did it feel good.

"You sure about this?" I sat back on my heels.

She gave me a sexy little smirk. "Are you?"

"I'm serious, Charlotte." And I was. I didn't want her to do something she was going to regret. This night could change a lot for us. "We still have to work together, and I know you'll be leaving soon. I just want to make sure—"

"I know what I want, Luke. I want you." She sat up and quickly tugged her shirt over her head before tossing it on the blanket next to us. "I don't want to think about anything else right now."

"Okay," I said, never one to second-guess a woman

whose mind was made up.

Charlotte liked to remind me daily that she was an independent woman who made her own decisions. This was one that I wasn't going to question. Especially when I got a glimpse of her in that lacy scrap of fabric she called a bra, and the matching panties I found when she lifted her hips and let me slide her jeans off.

"God, you're beautiful," I said, dropping my lips to the upper swell of her breasts.

I pulled my shirt off, wanting to feel my skin against hers. Her eyes went wide as I lowered myself onto her. The feel of her hands on my chest was searing as she smoothed them over it for the first time. As we explored each other's bodies, I committed the moment to memory. Not that I'd be able to forget it if I tried.

I popped the front clasp of her bra and freed her tits from the lace. Her rosy nipples tightened. Placing my lips around one and tugging it slightly with my teeth, I caressed the other between my fingertips.

She moaned, pursing her lips to muffle the sounds as I lavished attention on one and then the other. When her body rocked against mine and my name came out in a whisper of desperation, I knew right then that I needed to hear her scream it into the moonlight.

"We're in the middle of nowhere, baby," I said, slipping my hand down the front of her panties and finding the warm, wet heat I knew would be waiting for me. I deftly parted her folds and found the one spot that would drive her wild. "You be as loud as you want to be."

When she let out a little whimper of satisfaction, I swirled my thumb over the bundle of nerves, loving the way she took a deep breath and froze as I worked her aching flesh.

A sweet pink blush spread over her cheeks as she whispered, "Someone will hear."

I shook my head. "Right now, it's only you and me. Now, did you want me to suck on your pretty pink clit?"

"Yes," she murmured, but she looked too cute, too perfect like this, and I wasn't willing to give it up so easily.

I made to move my hand away from her. "I don't think I heard you. Maybe I should—"

She grabbed my wrist and guided me back between her thighs. "Please. Don't stop. I want you. I want to feel you there."

"Then all you need to do is scream."

I offered her what I hoped was a tantalizing grin, then guided her back against the blanket and dropped my lips to her pert, rosy nipples again. Taking one in my mouth, I rolled the tip of my tongue around the peak, mirroring the move of my thumb against her other straining bud.

She let out a little gasp and cried out, "Luke!"

As a reward, I pushed one finger inside her and closed my eyes as her walls quaked around it. Another rush of blood and need surged to my cock, making it pulse against the cutting zipper of my jeans, but I ignored it. Right now, this was all about Charlotte—hearing her scream, needing her to call my name.

I pushed another finger inside and she jerked against my movement, urging me to give her more.

"Yes," she hissed. "Luke, yes."

I sucked harder on her nipple, knowing that I might mark her with my teeth, but somehow that thought made me even more rock-hard than before. The idea of watching her tits bounce while I fucked her and looking at the spot where I'd claimed her as mine . . .

Fuck, I couldn't think of a single thing sexier than that.

"Please, I want to feel you, Luke," she cried out.

I pumped my fingers in and out as she rocked against my hand. Her hips lifted and writhed as I worked inside her, and I sucked harder against her skin, willing myself to focus on anything other than how good she felt, how ready.

But it was impossible. Here in the moonlight with all of nature around us, she was prettier and more perfect than I could have imagined. If I didn't free my cock and fuck her soon, I was going to explode.

When she begged, "Luke, please," I released her nipple with a little pop and kissed my way down her stomach, raking my nails over her sensitive skin with my free hand. Lowering myself down her body, I pushed my fingers even deeper inside as her channel quaked and crashed around me, then pressed my lips to her pretty pink bud.

"Oh my . . ." The last word was drowned out by a sharp gasp as my tongue swept out to tease her.

Gently, I used the tip of my tongue to draw little figure eights over her, and she wriggled beneath my touch, her hips bucking into my mouth as I fucked her with my fingers over and over again.

I knew it wasn't enough. She wanted more, wanted everything. Just like I did. But tonight, we would both have to wait a little longer.

When I finally gripped myself and pushed inside her, it was going to be perfect. Almost as perfect as she looked right here and now.

The moonlight shone on her creamy skin as I looked up at her, meeting her gaze as I lashed her bud again with my tongue.

"I can't wait to see what you look like when you come," I murmured, and then sucked her clit gently as she rocked into me again. "Does your mouth open in a cute little *o*?"

"Do you want me to show you?" She grasped the blanket on either side of her, and the walls of her pussy quaked around my fingers again, harder and tighter than before.

"No," I ground out. "I want to feel it."

This was the moment—my one shot to get it right.

Pulling my fingers from her, I said, "Keep going."

At my gruff command, she took the lead, her deft fingers circling her bud while I made quick work of shoving down my boxers and pulling a condom over my shaft. Watching her was the sexiest thing I'd ever seen.

"Hurry," she begged, and her eyes squeezed shut. "I'm so close."

I pulled her panties aside before shoving myself so deep inside that her breath caught, and I was pushed almost to the breaking point. That hot, tight channel squeezed me so tightly, I let out a groan.

All around me, she shuddered with pleasure. Her

hands returned to the blanket, tugging at it as she writhed against me. It was all so intense—the warm wetness of her pussy, the straining ache of my cock, and more than anything else, the fierce, desperate need for more.

With every little shiver of movement, there was an instant of gratification, a sliver of pleasure, but that hunger grew too, gnawing at my insides and begging me to lose control. I wanted desperately to fuck her harder, to take her in my arms and thrust so deep and fast, she wouldn't be able to breathe.

"Fuck yeah, baby." I leaned back and grabbed her thighs, watching as her tits bounced up and down with every thrust.

Briefly, I wondered what it would look like for me to come on those perfect tits of hers, my pearly seed coating her creamy white skin.

Then her mouth dropped into a little *o*, just as I'd hoped it would, and I wasn't thinking anything at all. She shuddered, murmuring my name under her breath.

With another shiver of pleasure at the sight, I gripped her harder still and demanded, "Scream for me, duchess."

It didn't take much convincing.

"Luke!" she cried, and her voice echoed back to us through the night air. "Luke!"

"Yes, baby, scream."

"Fuck me," she cried, and that was enough to send me over the edge.

Cupping one breast, I pinched her nipple as she bucked and trembled beneath me. God, she was beautiful, her perfect face tense with her need, her breast silky soft in my hand, and her tight cunt hugging me like a fist. The shivers of her orgasm were still rolling over her as mine came to the cliff and paused at the edge.

As I looked down at Charlotte in the moonlight, my cock glossy with her wetness as I pushed and pulled our bodies together, it was enough to make my balls ache, locked and ready for takeoff.

Quickly, I pulled her knees up to my chest and took her deeper, closing my eyes as the wet warmth of her sent a shiver through my veins, and my climax built. A low, deep groan was ripped from my lips as the gnawing pressure in my gut intensified, then loosened and spread through my body, sending frissons of satisfaction through me as hot streams spurted from my swollen length.

As the final waves of pleasure crashed down over me, I had only one thought.

We need to do this again . . .

And again and again.

Chapter Ten

Charlotte

Friday morning, I awoke in Luke's massive four-poster bed. Its blue sheets were twisted and disheveled, bearing the evidence of our lovemaking from last night, round two once we ended up here after leaving that magical hilltop.

His side of the bed was empty, and I could hear noises downstairs. Stretching leisurely, I noted my body felt tender and used in all the best ways. Luke made love with the same passion and intensity that he lived his life—he was wild, strong, and a bit hotheaded. I'd enjoyed myself immensely last night.

These last few days spent exploring each other's worlds were better than I could have dreamed. The most shocking revelation was that I'd gotten a taste of country life and I didn't hate it. The people, the food, the pace, the lifestyle—all were things I wasn't used to. But here in Shady Grove, I was learning to slow down and enjoy each moment, to savor each day. As unexpected as it was, I suspected I was learning a life lesson in the process.

But as much fun as I'd had with Luke, I already knew that our fling had a ticking clock attached to it. Eventually, the alarm would sound and it would all be over—I'd go back to my world, and he to his. A little pang of guilt flared inside me—I hadn't told him how I'd ended up here, or what I was running from. Now that we'd been intimate, I felt like my omission had been a bald-faced lie. But then again, maybe I didn't have to spill my guys about the whole messy affair. Luke had a past too, and I didn't pry into that. I respected his boundaries. Maybe we could both keep our secrets safely guarded and enjoy this for what it was.

I shrugged on a T-shirt and made my way downstairs. A hulking male form was standing near the coffeemaker, dressed in nothing more than a pair of worn jeans, but when he turned I saw it was Duke.

A slow smile unfurled on his lips. "Come give me some sugar."

Placing one hand on my hip, I stopped next to the counter, grabbing a coffee mug from the strainer by the sink. "I'm on to you, mister."

He chuckled. "Damn. I was just about to apologize for my performance last night."

"I know the difference between a man who's fucking with me and a man who's actually fucked me. And your brother did a real good job. Nice try, Duke." I patted his head.

The twins were virtually identical in every way, from their expressive green eyes with flecks of gold to their full mouths that pulled easily and often into a smirk. They were built exactly the same—six feet of hard muscle.

"You and Molly are the only people on the planet who can tell us apart. Even our own mother couldn't do it half the time," he added, still grinning at me.

I couldn't put my finger on exactly what it was, but even from that first day, I could tell who was who. It might sound like new-age nonsense, but maybe it was their auras. Where Duke was all playful and mischievous energy, Luke was all brooding, masculine intensity. The sexy stranger captured my attention from the first moment I saw him, even though I needed a man like I needed a new Louis Vuitton bag.

A few minutes later, Luke made his way into the kitchen and Duke excused himself, leaving us alone.

"Morning," Luke murmured, his gaze traveling the length of my bare legs.

"Come here," I told him. "I've got something to show you."

I tugged him toward the kitchen table, and over coffee, laid out my marketing plan. Luke sat back with a slight grin on his lips, listening attentively to every word.

"I'm impressed that you saw straight through Duke's game," he said.

My gaze flicked up to meet his. "I'd never make that mistake now that . . ."

"Now that what, duchess? I've been inside you?"

His voice was low and seductive, and a hot shiver raced through me. I lifted my chin, waiting for the press of his lips against mine.

"I'm just getting started," he whispered, treating me to a tender kiss.

Last night had been magical. Making love under the stars, and the way Luke took care of all my pleasure first before seeking his own. It was incredible.

Part of me wanted to pretend that this was real, but the looming end of my stay here was quickly approaching. And the past I was on the run from . . . Well, I had a bad feeling that it would catch up to me sooner or later.

"I could listen to you talk business all day, duchess."

I grinned at Luke. "Good, because I'm just getting started too."

Chapter Eleven

Luke

I could have listened to Charlotte ramble on all day long about search-engine optimization, whatever the hell that was. Seeing how passionate she was about the whole marketing thing was a real turn-on. She'd worked on the plan while we ate pancakes that morning, and hadn't let up since.

That was after I caught my brother trying to pull a fast one on her. After sneaking out of bed for a quick shower that morning, I went down to the kitchen and found her chatting with Duke while wearing one of my T-shirts like a nightgown.

The naturalness of the situation had stopped me in my tracks. Her long, toned legs peeking out from the shirt and her cute little bare feet on the hardwood floor were a sight I wouldn't have minded seeing every day, but that wasn't what we'd agreed to. Whatever we were doing here had an expiration date, and I needed to remember that.

I'd waited in the stairwell to remind myself that this couldn't last when I heard them talking. Duke would never actually make a move on her—we had a bro code that forbade it. I knew he was just seeing how invested she was in whatever it was we had going on.

But when I heard her call him out on not being me from the get-go, the squeeze on my heart was unexpected. And the stroke to my ego was like a balm to my soul.

"I know the difference between a man who's fucking with me and a man who's actually fucked me. And your brother did a real good job."

I'd fucked her, all right. And it was goddamn spectacular. I could still feel the tight squeeze of her around me. Just thinking about the past twenty-four hours had me ready to go again. If I only had Charlotte until her car was fixed, I was going to make the most of it. I'd let her eat and get a little work in first, though.

"They taught you all of this in college?" I asked, stopping her in mid-sentence.

"Some of it," she said with a grin. "Marketing changes so much every year. Every day, even. A lot of it I picked up along the way or learned on the fly."

"I'm impressed." I placed my hand on hers.

The urge to sweep my hand across the table—clearing it dramatically of her paperwork—was strong. I'd already had her on the ground under the stars, and in my bed, so adding a table to the list seemed like a mighty fine idea.

"I actually learned a lot from watching my father," she said.

Well, that abruptly put the brakes on the sexual nature of my thoughts. Nothing like the mention of dear old Dad to kill the mood. I nodded and told my dick to stand down.

"Not that he would ever know," she added, "or even let me get a word in at his firm."

"Why wouldn't he want you to be a part of it? You're smart, and like I said, you know your shit. Plus, you're his daughter."

She frowned. "Dad's firm is a real boys' club. I don't think he even took me seriously when I majored in marketing. I spent a lot of time trying to impress him and gain his approval. I'm done with that, though. He was never going to make room for me at Freemont and

Associates."

"That's ridiculous," I told her, feeling overprotective. I knew a little bit about parents disappointing you.

Her dad sounded like a grade-A asshole, which went a long way toward explaining why she was packed up and headed for LA. How on earth her father couldn't take her seriously was beyond me. I could see the frustration and disappointment in her eyes. Charlotte might have been trying to play it cool, but I could see the wound was still fresh.

"It's his loss."

"And your gain, Mr. Wilder," she said playfully.

"Is it ever." I rose up enough in my seat to lean over the table and plant my lips on hers. "You taste like maple syrup."

When I flicked my tongue across her lips, she lifted her eyebrows. "You wanna take that bottle up to your room and have a little fun?"

"That sounds like a real good idea. But didn't you say something about needing to check in with Wayne?"

"Oh, yeah." She deflated a little, looking disappointed. "I totally forgot about my car."

I wished I'd forgotten.

She picked up her phone from the table as I sat back down. After a quick swipe of her finger and a couple of taps, she put it up to her ear.

"Hello, this is Charlotte Freemont. I was calling to touch base with Wayne about my car." There was a pause as she listened. "So, he's out for the day?" She nodded a couple of times. "All right then. Thank you."

"No go?" I said, hoping the answer was just that.

"No go. Apparently, there's some kind of game tonight, and he's taken the day off to prepare."

Of course. Tonight was the first game of the high school football season.

"Yeah, the Stallions kick off tonight at seven. Wayne's kid is a senior this year. I'm sure he's on the starting roster."

She scratched her head and wrinkled her nose. She

had no idea what I was talking about.

"Shady Grove High School has their first game tonight," I explained. "Everyone in town treats it as a holiday. Football is a big deal around here, if you haven't figured that out yet."

"I guess so. You taking me to the game tonight?"

"You want to go?"

I was surprised, especially when she hadn't complained about Wayne's incompetence or the fact that her car still wasn't ready. And now she wanted to go to a football game with me? This girl sure knew how to keep me on my toes.

"I think I do." She nodded. "What time does it start?"

"Seven. That give you enough to primp?" I teased.

"More than enough."

She slipped from her seat and walked over to me. When she planted her perfect ass on my lap and wrapped her arms around my neck, she had my full attention.

"In fact," she said in a low voice, "that's more than enough time."

She ran her mouth up my jawline before taking the lobe of my ear between her lips and sucking gently. I swallowed hard as every drop of my blood rushed south.

"Why don't you grab that bottle and meet me upstairs, Mr. Wilder."

The purr of her words had my head spinning, but I wasn't completely dumbstruck. When she hopped up off my lap and started for the stairs, I grabbed the syrup bottle and followed her.

We had a few hours to kill before kickoff, and enough syrup to make each of them sweeter than the last.

• • •

The roar of the crowd was deafening. The Stallions were up by six, but the opposing team had the ball with three minutes to go.

Charlotte turned wide eyes on me. "This is insanity."

"If they make it to the end zone, it's going to be even

worse," I warned.

The Stallions were heavy favorites this year, and losing their first game would have been a huge upset. The crowd was screaming out their defensive chants, reminding the players on the field of the pressure that was on them.

That was one thing I didn't miss about playing football—the constant pressure to win.

Somewhere between playing in high school and when I played in college, the fun went out of the game for me. I wasn't sad at all for my football career to be over, and neither was my body, which had been battered and bruised through my entire adolescence. Not that I could ever share that with anyone in my hometown. That was akin to blasphemy in a football town. You either played football, or wanted to be playing.

"I want one of those giant pretzels," Charlotte said. "I'm going to go now while everyone is watching this. There's no line."

I had to laugh at her indifference to the game. There we were in the middle of a nail-biter, and she wanted a pretzel.

"I'll go with you," I said, taking her hand in mine.

"You sure? Don't you want to see what happens?"

"I'm good," I told her as we stood up and headed down the bleachers. "I've seen enough football games to last me a lifetime."

As we walked down the metal steps, she wrapped her free hand around my arm and pressed herself against my side.

"Is this how high school was for you?" she asked. "Friday-night lights and all that?"

"Yeah. Duke and I played. We even went to college on scholarship."

"That's awesome."

"It was all right." I shrugged. "Paid for college."

"You miss it? All the hype? The attention?"

"Not really." As soon as the words were out of my mouth, I half expected lightning to strike me where I stood.

"What about the cheerleaders? I'll bet they were all over you."

"There were a few," I said with a chuckle. "I had some good times underneath these bleachers."

"Is that right?"

A spark of jealousy flickered in her eyes, and before I could say another word, Charlotte tugged me underneath the bleachers, her pretzel forgotten.

Her lips were on mine before I could even register what was happening. The stomps and screams coming from above us grew louder with each tick of the clock, but all I could do was concentrate on the beautiful woman pressing her body against mine. Her lips and tongue were doing their damnedest to erase any memories of high school make-out sessions under the bleachers that might have been lingering in my head.

And it was working.

I grabbed one of the metal support rods above my head and steadied us as I wrapped the other arm around her waist. You'd think after our morning with the maple syrup, she would have had her fill of me, but here we were, making out under the bleachers like two sex-starved teenagers.

"You forget about them yet?" She smirked at me when we finally broke for air, both of us trying to catch our breath.

"Baby, they were never even a memory." I dropped a last quick kiss on her lips. "Now, let's get that pretzel and get the hell out of here."

Chapter Twelve

Charlotte

The crowd thundered overhead as Luke grabbed my hand, pulling me to the edge of the bleachers where people were already pouring from the stands.

"Shit," he mumbled. "Game must be over."

"Does that mean the concession stand is closed?"

He laughed when my stomach grumbled. "How is that even louder than the people around us?"

I shrugged. "Special talent, I guess."

Luke led me by the hand as we blended into the crowd, weaving through the mass of people heading back to their cars. Here and there, I caught people looking at him from the corner of their eyes, their expressions half-adoring, half-confused—probably because they were trying to make out which twin he was.

Our earlier conversation about football came to mind. He'd really downplayed it, I knew, but it had to be no small thing to get a full ride to college, especially for a school as high profile as A&M. And in a town like this? It would likely make him some kind of god. Still, he took it in stride, smiling at the people around him and ignoring their grins of approval and adoration.

"What happened after college?" I asked when we finally made it through the thick of the crowd.

The concession stand was just in front of us, and Luke pivoted to look at me.

"What?"

"You said you went to A&M for college. What did you do after that? I mean, what did you major in? Did you always want to run the distillery?"

His face twisted for a minute, but as we came to the front of the little snack shack, he smiled and waved at the girl behind the counter who was tossing out the leftover hot dogs.

"Jill," he said. "Hey."

She blinked up at him, and when she realized who he was, she blushed. "Hey there."

"Got any leftover pretzels, or did you toss those out already?"

She nodded and headed for the case where five giant golden-brown pretzels twirled on a silver rack. Taking a paper tissue, she grabbed one and held it out for him.

"Hell of a game," she said. "Almost like when you were playing. 'Cept, of course, if you'd been out there, we would've won."

She nodded toward the back wall, and my gaze followed hers to a row of framed jerseys. Okay, so apparently downplaying didn't quite cover it.

Five jerseys hung from the white cinderblock wall, all displayed under a bright yellow light. In the very center were two that read "Wilder," one I assumed with Luke's number and the other with Duke's.

"It was a great game. They gave it all they had," Luke said, seemingly oblivious to my revelation. "What do I owe you?"

Jill shrugged. "On the house. Would've gone in the trash, anyway."

We said our good-byes before joining the crowd still streaming to the parking lot. When I took a bite of the salty hot dough, Luke frowned at me.

"Don't you want some mustard or cheese?"

"And sully the perfect taste of this pretzel? Not on your life." I gave him a playful shove and took another bite, thinking over what to say next. I knew what I *wanted* to say.

Don't take me back to the inn. Let me stay at your place tonight, and tomorrow night too. And then we can just go our separate ways and have this fun memory to take with us.

Still, it felt too forward. I couldn't exactly invite myself into someone else's home for the weekend, and even if I could ... wasn't that a little too serious for something that we both agreed was a fling?

"Charlotte?"

I shook my head, trying to recall what Luke had been saying, but it was no use. "Huh?"

"I said, can I give you a ride to the inn?"

"Oh, yeah, that would be great." I followed him to his truck, listening to the chatter around us as people rehashed the game.

"What were we talking about?" he asked as he got behind the wheel.

I settled into the passenger seat. "I asked about college. What did you major in?"

"Business."

"For the distillery?"

His face twisted into a frown. "Not exactly."

"What does that mean?"

He glanced at me from the corner of his eye, his profile and square jaw looking as fine as hell, even in the darkened interior of the truck. "I'll tell you, but first you have to promise that you're not the jealous type."

"Jealous?" I laughed, but my stomach tightened. "What do you mean?"

"You know what jealousy looks like. Promise me you can contain yourself."

"I think I can manage." I rolled my eyes, but secretly I was wishing I was anywhere else right now.

"I had actually gone to school for business because my girlfriend at the time wanted to open a high-end spa," he explained.

I rose my eyebrows but said nothing.

"She was a real city type, and we had a plan to open her company in Dallas because that's where the clientele was. But things didn't work out that way."

"What do you mean?"

"By the time I graduated, the distillery was going under, and my dad was too. I had to come back home to lend a hand."

I shot him a glance under my lashes, a twinge of pity sizzling through me at the pain in his voice. "And Duke did the same?"

Luke nodded. "No-brainer."

"And what happened to . . ." I let the question hang in the air, studying Luke's face as I waited for him to fill in the blank. He didn't look pained anymore, but he didn't look excited to be dredging it all up either.

"Sarah," he finished for me. "She came back with me. For a while, at least. Like I said, she was the city type, and living in a small town—especially one where everyone already knew me—wasn't her style."

"I see." I nodded. "That must have been hard for you. Taking on everything and—"

"Looks like we're here." Luke cut me off as he pulled in front of the inn.

I stared at it, stunned we'd gotten here so quickly.

Why did time seem to fly by so quickly when I was with him?

"Okay then. Well, thanks for that and the pretzel," I said, shaking it at him like a stick. "I had fun."

I moved to push my door open and paused, sucking in a steadying breath before turning to face Luke.

"Do you want to come in for a while?"

Chapter Thirteen

Luke

Charlotte glanced from me to the inn and back again before tilting her head to the side, letting her silky hair cascade over her shoulder. "Don't feel obligated or anything. I just thought I'd ask. No big deal." Her cheeks went pink as she scrabbled for the door handle again.

"I'll come in for a sec." My groin went tight and I shrugged. "But only to help you pack," I said softly.

She blinked in confusion, her mouth half-open. "What do you mean?"

I leaned closer and traced a finger over the line of her jaw. "Your car isn't going to be fixed until Monday. It's just plain silly for you to keep staying here when I'd rather have you in my bed." I let out a low growl, leaning in to nip at her earlobe before pulling back.

She dropped the last bit of her pretzel into her lap and let out a nervous laugh. "Are you sure about that?"

I nodded. "Look, we both know the deal here. You've got to get back to your life and I've got to focus on the distillery, but for the rest of the weekend . . ." I shrugged. "I don't see what's stopping us from having a little fun. Don't you like what we've been doing?"

Her eyes gleamed, and I guessed she was thinking—like I was—of the way I'd poured maple syrup all over her body that afternoon and lapped it up with my tongue. I was careful to ensure her nipples and the delicious spot between her legs were well and truly clean before I dragged her into the shower and lathered the rest of her body with shampoo.

"It's been fun," she said, sounding a little breathless.

"So, it's settled. Let's go get your stuff."

She quirked her lips to the side before picking up her pretzel and pushing open her door. "Fine. I'll grab my bag, but you stay here. I don't want anyone seeing me leave with you and getting the wrong idea that I'm a woman of loose morals," she said with a chuckle. "But I'm warning you, if you're going to tease me like this, you'd better be ready to hurry back to your place and make good on those implied threats."

"You got it."

I grinned and watched her disappear behind the inn's front door, my mind drifting to how she'd looked beneath the bleachers and in my oversized T-shirt this morning, compared to how she looked when she first got here.

There was no use in comparing, of course, but it seemed like there was something different about her now. Back when we first met, she was in hoity-toity, high-class New York mode. But under the bleachers, and in my bed, she wasn't a duchess. She was just Charlie, laughing and pretty, and all mine.

But then, Sarah had been like that too.

And Charlotte would be going soon, just like Sarah did, but this time I had the advantage of knowing that in advance. I wasn't serious about Charlotte like I'd been with my ex, and we both knew as much. So, as long as I kept my heart out of all this and just had fun, what was the big deal?

Molly had told me I worked too hard and needed a break. Maybe this was exactly what she meant—I needed a warm, sexy body to share my bed, someone I could have some laughs and unwind with, no strings attached. No harm, no foul.

Charlotte stepped out of the inn, suitcase in hand. I climbed out to help her with the bag, but she lugged it around the truck and shoved it inside with surprising speed. As we settled back into our seats and prepared to head back to my house, I sensed an odd disturbance in the air between us, a tension that hadn't been there before.

Of course, it could have been because she was getting ready to spend the rest of the weekend with a man she'd only known for a few days, but something told me that wasn't it.

Maybe I shouldn't have mentioned Sarah earlier. Or maybe when I did, I should have turned to watch Charlotte's expression to see exactly what she thought. If, of course, she had any thoughts about my ex at all. It had been so long ago, and my life had changed so much since then.

I cleared my throat. "Okay, so you know all about my life and my past. What about you?"

She reeled around to look at me. "Like what?"

"I told you about college and Sarah. You must have

some story about—I don't know—your debutante ball? The prince who asked for your hand in marriage?"

She blushed and looked out the window. "I didn't have a debutante ball."

"College then. You majored in marketing, right?"

"I did. Not much to know. I went to Sarah Lawrence. It was fine." She shrugged. "End of story, really."

"I doubt that. No guys in your life?" I raised my brows. "High school sweetheart who broke your heart?"

"I went to an all-girls school, but good try," she shot back.

"Huh. I don't know a single person in the world that ever stopped," I said with a grin. "You don't mean to sit here and tell me you gave your virginity to some random guy you met when your car broke down in Texas?"

She rolled her eyes. "Okay, so I've had boyfriends, but that doesn't mean they were anything interesting enough to talk about."

"What was the last one like? What was his name?"

"Why? You the jealous one now, Luke?" She shot me a tight grin. "You gonna go fight him?"

I laughed. "Depends on how things ended. Was he mean to you?"

She turned to look out the window again. "His name was Prescott."

This time I laughed even louder. "Are you for real?"

She blushed. "It was a family name."

"Which means he was actually Prescott Moneybags the what? Fourth? Fifth?"

"Prescott *Billingsley*." She cleared her throat and added under her breath, "The sixth."

"Wow, the sixth." I let out a low whistle. "So, he's old money then. Big score."

She frowned. "Like I said, nothing to write home about."

"You mean to tell me your parents didn't do a happy dance when you told them who you were dating?"

"Look, it's not important."

She rubbed her palms over her thighs, and I did my best not to roll my eyes.

"How did things end?"

Another heavy silence filled the cab of the truck, and she shifted in her seat. "It was fine. Things just didn't work out. Look, I don't want to talk about it," she practically snapped, then smoothed a hand over her hair. "I'm sorry. You were so open. I shouldn't—"

"No, no." I shook my head. "It's fine. If you don't want to talk about it, we don't have to."

I couldn't deny, though, that her replies intrigued me and sent my sixth sense tingling. While I wasn't jealous, exactly, I was much more invested in her answers than I should have been.

This is a fling, Luke. Don't forget it.

I gripped the wheel more tightly and turned my attention back to the road. "Look, I normally meet a couple of old friends at the bar after the game, but I can call and cancel if you'd rather not go—"

"No, don't cancel. You had no way of knowing I'd be here, and I don't want you to bail. That said, I'm really tired. Why don't you just drop me off? I'll get a nice up-close-and-personal look at that big claw-foot tub of yours, and have some popcorn. A nice little 'me' night."

The image of her shimmering with water as she stood from the bathtub, her pearly-white skin free of a towel, made another rush of need surge to my cock, but I nodded all the same. Suddenly, I felt like I needed the space.

"Okay, if you're sure. I won't stay out long."

"I'm sure."

I dropped her off and headed for the bar, thinking about Sarah . . . and Prescott Billingsley the Sixth.

Prescott was exactly the kind of name for a guy like that. The ritzy New York royalty that she'd inevitably marry someday. Then, when they had their penthouse and she slid into their claw-foot tub, maybe she'd think about the one in my house and remember . . .

Or maybe not.

Either way, it didn't matter. This thing we had? It had an expiration date stamped on it, and nobody was more okay with that than me. Charlotte was probably itching to get back to city life, and Lord knew I had enough to do with the distillery to keep me busy for another few years at least.

It was a shame, though. If she were something else, someone else ... if she were the girl who'd pulled me beneath the bleachers earlier tonight? Well, I might have been able to fall in love with someone like that.

• • •

When I got to the Drunk Skunk, it didn't take me long to find Case and Ranger already bellied up to the bar and waiting with a third beer in front of the empty stool beside them. As I made my way nearer, Case made a whooping sound and Ranger patted the stool.

"The prodigal quarterback returns," Ranger said. "Why are you so late?"

"I had to grab Charlotte's stuff and drop her off."

"Oh, she headed out of town tonight?" Case asked, but Ranger cut in before I had the chance to answer.

"Of course not. You know Wayne was at the game."

"Which means if she's not at the inn and she's not out of town . . ." Case eyed me as he pieced it all together. "Aw, shit."

"Shut up," I muttered, but Ranger hooted again.

"Sure you want to spend your night with us when you got better prospects waiting for you at home?"

"This is why nobody tells you anything," I said, and then took a swig of my beer.

"People tell us plenty." Case shrugged. "Just depends if we care to listen."

"Did you see this one?" Ranger asked Case.

He bit his knuckle and nodded. "She's pretty. Real nice figure. Would've pegged her for Duke's type if I hadn't heard about the whole salon debacle."

"Something happened at the salon?" I raised my eyebrows, trying to act nonchalant but curious anyway, and also oddly irritated by Case's notice of Charlotte's figure. He wasn't blind, after all, and she did have a banging body, but still.

"Yep, heard it from Audrey. Mrs. French always gets her nails done on Mondays, but apparently Charlotte walked in and took her spot. Got her hair done too in some fancy blowout, whatever the hell that means."

"I don't know how any of that has anything to do with me," I shot back.

"A girl whose first goal in town is to get her nails and hair done? Big-city type with some designer handbag? Doesn't ring a bell?" Ranger raised his eyebrows and my stomach twisted.

"Look, if you're talking about Sarah—"

Case grimaced. "God, I hope nobody is. I'm trying to have a beer and enjoy my night. No need to relive that nightmare."

"She wasn't that bad," I argued, although I inwardly cringed at the memory.

It was true, Sarah had stuck out around Shady Grove about as much as . . . well, about as much as Charlotte did. But there were differences between the two. Sarah would never have gone to the game with me tonight, and she sure as shit would have minded if I'd wanted to hang out with the guys instead of spending time with her. And she never would have eaten a concession-stand pretzel.

Still, that was the girl I'd thought I wanted to marry. I'd had the ring and everything. In fact, I still had it, tucked away in a drawer along with the note she'd left behind.

But Charlotte wasn't Sarah. This was a totally different situation and would have a totally different outcome.

I raised a hand to put an end to the debate. "I'm with Case on this one. Why don't we just have some beers and cool it with all the girl talk? That was a hell of a game tonight, after all."

Lucky for me, the guys sensed I'd had enough, and turned the subject to tonight's game. They dissected each of the plays and went over the stats of the star athletes for each team. The Stallions, we all agreed, would do better next week.

Although I tried to immerse myself in the stats and reasoning for every play, I still found myself thinking of

Charlotte, and about how I would feel when, two days from now, she climbed into her car and got back to her life. I wanted her to remember me, even if we couldn't be together. To take a piece of me with her when she went.

If I were being honest, I wanted her to leave a piece of herself behind too. Something for me to remember and hold on to when I thought about what could have been between us.

You know ... if we weren't totally wrong for each other.

Chapter Fourteen

Charlotte

Luke didn't wake me on Saturday morning, and neither did the bright, glittery sunshine that poured through the windows of his bedroom. Instead, the phone that I had fallen asleep beside buzzed so close to my face that I shot bolt upright, my heart racing as I frantically glanced around.

I clutched my chest, then let out a deep breath and grabbed for the damned thing, checking to make sure I hadn't disturbed Luke. But no, he slept on like a log, snoring gently with his mouth halfway open.

I reached toward him, tempted to brush back a tuft of his mussed hair, but then my phone buzzed again and he shifted, swatting it away from him as he snuggled deeper into the sheets.

Reaching quickly, I grabbed the phone just before it tipped over the edge of the bed, then glanced down at the flashing screen. I had so many missed calls and follow-up voice mails that a knot formed in my stomach at the sheer number alone.

Breathing deeply through my nose, I eased from the bed and tiptoed out of the room, careful to close the door quietly behind me before edging my way into the kitchen and opening the dreaded screen.

Okay, all I had to do was look at the last five calls. That was it. If I wanted to listen to them, I would. If not? They could wait for another day.

With another deep breath, I sucked in my cheeks and scanned the list of names.

Mom.

Dad.

Valentina.

A number I didn't recognize.

Prescott.

I did a double-take at the last name, hating the little heart emoji that still lingered beside his name in my contact list, and deleted the message without listening. Okay, that was one decision down. All I had to do now was decide on the rest.

Better to start soft, right? Crawl before you run?

I tapped Valentina's name and held the phone to my ear.

"Charlotte, hey. Just calling to see what the deal is with the car and the town and everything. I hope you're on the road. Can't wait to see you!" She made a happy little screeching noise, and then the message clicked off.

Okay, that wasn't so bad. I glanced at the list again and chose my next poison—the number I didn't recognize. Even a bill collector or heavy breather would likely be better than a message from my mother.

"Ms. Freemont, this is Dr. Maloney. I'm sorry to be calling you out of the blue like this, but your parents told me that there might be some cause for concern. Could you please call me back and let me know if you're all right, and where you are? Your parents are very worried, and I would like to get you the help you need and deserve." He left his number and then hung up.

I stared at the phone, blinking at it like it had slapped me.

Was that a ... psychiatrist? Did they think, just because I didn't want to marry Prescott or stick around in their plastic little world, that I was having some kind of mental breakdown?

But then, I had fled the scene without a word and headed for California. That would worry any parent, I was sure. Even if my mom's Botoxed face was no longer capable of expressing emotion, surely there was a heart left rattling somewhere in that impossibly narrow chest cavity of hers.

Conflicted, I clicked on the next message and listened.

"Charlotte, darling, it's me." My mom's voice floated over the line, airy and light, as if she were calling to see if I was available for tea this afternoon. *"I know you must be in a state right now. You probably think you've ruined everything, and I won't lie. It is a little tough around the club,"* she said with a cluck of her tongue that set my teeth on edge. *"But you have to remember other girls have still made worse mistakes. Remember when Nina Weiss's daughter ran away and eloped with that boy she met on the subway, of all places? Anyway, what I'm saying is come home. Prescott and Daddy will forgive you. Just come home and forget this momentary lapse."*

The message ended and I looked down at the phone again. She hadn't asked if I was okay—hadn't even asked where I was. Though, of course, I knew why.

It didn't matter. Or it wouldn't until I was exactly where they told me to be.

"Well, better make the rounds of it," I mumbled and held up the phone to listen to my dad's message.

There was a long moment of silence, then the sound of men laughing and the clicking of glasses followed by low chatter. Someone said something that was too muffled to make out, and Dad replied in a booming voice, *"So then Duff says, you think that's bad, you should see the other guy!"* More laughter followed, and I clicked the message off without waiting to hear the other forty-three seconds.

My father had butt-dialed me. As far as he knew, I was missing and heartbroken, and he was out somewhere drinking and laughing with his buddies, telling tired old stories?

I set my jaw, trying to ignore the sting, and scrolled down to find another message from my mother. I clicked on it more out of righteous anger than interest, and when her voice floated over the line again, I gritted my teeth, waiting for her to ask me this time where I was, or if I was okay.

"Charlotte, honey, it's me again. I wanted you to know I've paid everyone from the reception and that's all handled. I've also arranged for you to see a few doctors, so they should be calling you in short order. I hope to see you soon."

She hoped to see me soon? That was *it*?

No I love you?

No nothing?

My mother's only concern was for her checkbook—and her image. And that was exactly why I'd escaped—and exactly why I hadn't told Luke about my past. I didn't want him believing I was some silly society girl who only cared about the label stitched into her clothes or the number of zeroes in her bank account. I wasn't like them. *I wasn't.* And even though I knew that I shouldn't have lied to Luke when he asked me about Prescott, I just wanted so badly to believe that all of that was behind me, and never speak of it again.

I slammed my phone on the kitchen table and huffed out a sigh, blinking back angry, frustrated tears.

I was just about to slam it again, just for the satisfaction of it, when a deep male voice behind me made me jump.

"Early to bed, early to rise, I guess," Luke murmured, looping his arms around me and pulling me back against his chest.

I could feel the long, rigid outline of his cock against my ass. It was amazing how just the feel of his heated skin could mellow the fury in my chest while unfurling a whole other kind of heat inside me.

"What was all that about?" He nodded toward my phone, and I shook my head.

"Nothing. Checking for word about the car." The lies were coming quicker and easier, and I hated myself for that, but there was no sense in dragging him into my drama when I was leaving in two days.

"I'm guessing it's not ready by that reaction. I hate to say it, but I wouldn't hold your breath on hearing about that anytime soon."

"I know, I know. It's Saturday, so Wayne's drunk." I rolled my eyes. "It doesn't take long to learn the ins and outs of a place like this."

He stiffened and paused, still in the process of nuzzling my hair. "Something wrong with that?"

I wanted to bite my tongue off. "Not at all," I said, shaking my head. "What does Saturday normally look like for you?"

"When there's a beautiful woman in my house, I tend not to leave the bed. Especially since she was asleep when I got home last night." He laced his fingers with mine and spun me around to face him. "What do you say, beautiful? Want to go get dirty together?"

"I'd say that would be perfect," I murmured as he leaned in to kiss me, but I put my finger on his lips, calling on every bit of my willpower to hold him in place. "If we didn't have so much work to do. You said you wanted my help, and I want to help you. Now tell me, where do you work best?"

With a long-suffering sigh and the promise of a reward when we were done, Luke arranged all the papers and forms I needed on his dining room table, and I settled in to work. For the next couple of hours, we pored over the papers and drew out designs.

When the morning became the afternoon, Luke disappeared into the kitchen to make us sandwiches, leaving me alone to take a break. I found myself glancing around his house, still sort of pinching myself that I was there.

It really was a sweet little place—bright and cheery with all the homey touches I would never have expected in a bachelor pad. It was a house built for a family, and as I stared around the table, I pictured tiny little Lukes sitting in those empty chairs, all joining hands and saying grace before their Sunday meal.

It was like a fantasy family life, certainly not anything I'd grown up with, and for the first time I felt a little envious of Luke. His parents were gone but he still had Duke and Molly, and the legacy of that early family life would always be with them. They could all still sit around this table, and if he went missing . . .

Well, there was no doubt that one of his loved ones would at least ask where he was.

My heart gave a squeeze and I gnawed on my lower lip, trying to push the thoughts of my family from my mind. Luckily, Luke reappeared a few seconds later and sat a turkey sandwich in front of me, the crusts cut off and the sandwich itself cut into four perfect triangles.

I laughed, my melancholy evaporating under the warmth of his boyish grin. "Wow, gourmet."

"Only the best for you, city girl."

There was no malice in his words, though, and I picked up the sandwich and bit in. It had been years since someone had made me a sandwich like this, but there was no denying the simple goodness.

He took a seat across from me and dug in as we talked. He told stories about his friends and the business, and about Duke and Molly. Suddenly, the image of all of us sitting around the table became even clearer in my mind, and I got so wrapped up in the flow of conversation that I found myself speaking before I stopped to think.

"What do you think the odds are of your wife having twins like you and Duke?" I asked, taking a hasty bite of my sandwich to distract from my reddening face.

Oh Lord, I'd really done it now. He was going to think I was some sort of loony stalker, naming our twins after what amounted to nothing more than a little fling.

He shot me a quizzical glance. "I don't know. Why do you ask?"

"No reason at all," I said brightly, shaking my head. "I just feel bad for her and her vag and all. Probably rough on the old girl, squeezing out doubles, you know?"

Luke laughed and then groaned. "Oh my God, that was funny until I had to think of it in terms of my own mom, so thanks for that."

It was better than the alternative, so I swept my arm out and executed a little half bow. "You're quite welcome. And there's plenty more where that came from. I'll be here all weekend."

Taking advantage of the reprieve from pure humiliation, I quickly shifted gears, steering the conversation back toward the safety of work again.

But then, as we worked and talked, Luke's chair

seemed to inch closer and closer to mine. As afternoon turned into evening, the sun that had shone through the wide windows was replaced with twinkling stars, and I lost focus of everything.

Everything ... except exactly how close he was sitting. How it would take nothing at all for him to close the space between us, slide our papers to the floor, and splay me out on the dining room table right then and there.

My cheeks heated as I imagined him spreading my legs open, his tongue laving me the way he had in the field that first night. Warmth spread through my body at the thought alone, and I squeezed my thighs together, not wanting to give in to the swell of need and longing. Not yet, anyway.

"Don't you think?" Luke asked.

I forced myself back to the present and nodded my head vigorously. "Oh, um, yeah. Yes. Definitely."

He leaned across me to write something on the file in front of me. His earthy, manly smell wafted up as he moved and I breathed in deeply, remembering the way that scent had tasted on his skin. With his sun-kissed hair in front of me, it was all I could do not to reach out and run my fingers through his locks, but again I refrained.

We're talking business. Tonight is about business.

My stomach rumbled, and I glanced at him from the corner of my eye.

"Hungry?" he asked, and I nodded. "What are you in the mood for?"

When he smiled at me, I wanted to blurt out the answer, the real answer—him. Maple syrup. Whipped cream. Whatever he would let me do, just so long as I could feel his body on mine again.

He was just so damn close.

"I don't know," I murmured, and he shrugged.

"Think it over."

I nodded again and he scooted his chair even closer, his knee brushing against mine as he moved. Another shot of pure electricity jolted through me at his touch.

What was it with him? It wasn't like I'd never been

with men before, but now every time I thought about his fingers on my body, I found myself panting and needy like never before.

I had to get it together—and fast. Not just because I was sure he could see the way my eyes dilated and fixed on his lips every time he spoke, but because . . . well, tomorrow was Sunday. We only had one more day together, and if I got used to feeling like this every time I was around him, what would I do when I was gone? When I finally had to leave?

"So, I was thinking about this for the logo," he said as he sketched something on the paper in front of me.

Focus, I told myself. *Focus. You promised you would help him.*

But I couldn't. All I could think about was the way the table would *thunk* against the hardwood while he held my hips and turned me over, ready to take me from behind.

Panic filled me at the realization that this might be the last time we were together. I wanted to make it special and—

"So, what do you think?" he asked.

I looked down at the paper to see a little stick-figure man and woman in a compromising position. I let out a short laugh, my cheeks flushing.

"Am I that obvious?"

His mouth quirked to the side. "Something like that. But luckily, great minds think alike."

His hand stroked my thigh, working its way to the inside of my leg, just above where I could already feel my panties getting wet.

"I actually have a better idea."

I plucked the pencil from his other hand and scribbled on the paper, just beneath his drawing. When I pulled my hand back, his gaze fell on the image of a stick-figure woman on her knees in front of a very happy-looking stick-figure man.

"Far be it for me to argue," he said and cupped the space between my thighs, rubbing gently before continuing. "Just know that I still want to fuck you after."

I knew Duke and Molly would be gone all day to

lend a hand to a neighbor, leaving us truly and completely alone. That feeling made me bold, a little reckless.

"If you insist," I teased, then sank to my knees in front of him as he kicked out his chair to face me.

With deft hands, he loosened the buckle and tugged his belt free, letting it drop to the floor with a loud clunk. Then he released the button and zipper and pulled his jeans to his ankles before kicking them aside until he was left in nothing but his black boxer briefs.

Already, I could see the huge bulge jutting out beneath the fabric, and my mouth watered at the idea of tasting him. Why had I waited so long for this? In the entire week we'd had, how had I wasted so much time? And now, with less than two days left . . .

Tomorrow I would have to do it again, just so I had more than one memory to take with me. And then maybe we could do it in the shower and—

But I was getting ahead of myself. Here and now was about him, pulling down those boxers to reveal the huge, hard cock I knew was waiting for me, wanting me. I licked my lips as he pulled his briefs down and tossed them aside with the rest of his clothes.

"Shirt too," I said, and he raised his eyebrows.

"When did you get so bossy?"

I stood and turned as if I were going to walk away. "Okay, if you don't want to listen."

Big, powerful hands gripped my hips and pulled me back against his muscular chest as he whispered into my ear, "You're not going anywhere."

My heart skipped a beat as he gripped the hem of my shirt and tugged it over my head. Unthinking, I followed his lead, stretching my hands over my head and letting my shirt join his clothing on the floor.

"I'll show you mine if you show me yours," he murmured.

My breath caught as, with the slightest twist, my bra tightened and then released as I allowed it to fall away from me.

"I want to see those tits bounce while you suck my dick," he said, and another surge of longing rushed between my thighs.

My heart was beating so fast and the blood was rushing to my ears with so much intensity that I wanted to fall to my knees in front of him and suck long and deep. I slid from his lap and took my place between his open knees, my thoughts filled with nothing but how hot his skin would feel against my hips, how amazing he would smell as I bobbed up and down.

He dragged his shirt up over his head and grinned at me, revealing a muscular chest and the sexiest set of abs I'd ever been up close and personal with. "A deal's a deal. Though I want you to take off those pants too. You'd look so hot with your knees open, sucking my cock and waiting for me."

I shivered a little at the thought, but the feistier side of me took over. "Not part of the deal. You've got to wait for that."

I inched closer to him, taking the base of his shaft in one hand while I cupped his balls with the other. Gently, I massaged him while I worked him up and down, readying him for me. There was no way I'd be able to fit all of him in my mouth—in truth, I might need both hands just to make up for the portion of him I wouldn't be able to take—but watching him as I worked was enough to make me want to come right then and there.

His eyes darkened as he watched. He tucked one hand under my chin to force me to look into those brooding, hungry eyes.

"You're a tease," he said, his voice low and gravelly.

I tossed him a smile. "You want my mouth?"

But I didn't wait for him to respond. As his hand moved to grasp the nape of my neck, I leaned down and took him into my mouth, sucking his sensitive head as I rolled the tip of my tongue over him. He let out a low groan as I worked and took him deeper, doing my best to fit as much of him inside my mouth as I could.

His skin was even hotter than I imagined, and as he bobbed against the back of my throat, my tongue burned with the sensation of lapping him. With a little tick of movement, I could feel him growing harder still inside my mouth, and he gripped the back of my neck with more force, urging me to keep up.

All the while, I worked him with one hand, loving the way his thighs twitched with every long, deep suck. With him still inside my mouth, I let out a little moan of approval, simultaneously loving and hating the ache in my jaw that was building with every passing thrust. My lips were becoming sore with sweet, sensitive heat, and I knew when I pulled away, they would be swollen and red from my efforts. This, I knew, would only make his kisses cooler by comparison in the best, most scintillating way.

That was, if he kissed me at all. For all I knew, he might simply bend me over the table and have his wicked way with me—just like his little stick figures had done.

"Enough," he groaned as his commanding grip dragged me back and away from him. "I can't fucking take it anymore. Take off those pants and let me see what's mine."

With the deep rumble of his voice, I knew better than to argue, even though I felt bereft the second my lips left him. Standing, I unzipped my jeans and stepped carefully out of them until I was in nothing but a bright blue scrap of lace. Silently, I hooked my thumbs under the elastic, but then Luke was on his knees in front of me, his teeth on my panties as he dragged them to the floor. When he righted himself, he kissed me between my thighs, and I let out another little shiver of pleasure.

"Bend over," he commanded, and again I followed his lead.

With one hand, I swept aside the papers we'd spent all day toiling over and then bent over the table, careful to pull myself onto my tiptoes so he could get a nice, good look at what I knew he wanted most to see.

"Fuck," he groaned. "I wish I could take a picture. I could stare at your pussy all day, baby."

I shot a smile at him from over my shoulder.

Apparently, that was all it took. With another muttered oath, he gripped himself and drove into me hard and fast, and I let out a little gasp.

His powerful fingers dug into my thighs, and with greedy, hungry thrusts, he bent my body to his will. With one hand on the table to steady me, I reached the other between my legs and pleasured myself, heightening the steady push and pull of his swollen cock as he drove into me harder and harder still.

"That's it, baby. I love watching you touch yourself,"

he rasped.

I looked over my shoulder to catch a glimpse of the steady concentration in his eyes. With every thrust, his jaw ticked with desperate need, and the sight of it alone made me let out a little moan of pleasure. If this was our last time together, I was going to make it memorable. I was going to make sure we came together.

Working myself faster still, I clenched around his huge length, and he let out another low groan.

"Fuck," he muttered, and I pushed back against him, causing him to take me even faster than before.

With every move, he pushed deeper inside me. I closed my eyes, savoring the way my inner walls tightened, shaking and quaking to the point of spilling over into orgasm.

I was so close, so close to the edge, and all I had to do was—

"Damn, Charlotte."

My name on his lips was like the key to a hidden room. A surge of euphoria rushed over me and I gripped the table with both hands, using it to steady myself as the orgasm ripped through my every cell. My channel closed over him, gripping and releasing in a flurry of spasms.

"Luke," I cried.

His fingers dug into my skin to the point of pain as he bucked against me, groaning and flexing as he came, but I didn't care. All I wanted was to feel him letting go, losing himself in me as I lost myself in him. Having everything, everything we could give each other.

Even if it was only for a little while.

Chapter Fifteen

Luke

"Shit." I rolled over and rubbed my eyes before glancing at the digital clock on my nightstand, all too aware that Charlotte was still curled next to me, her hair splayed across my blue pillowcase.

"What?" she mumbled as she reached for me, pulling me closer.

"I missed church."

"Just go to a later service."

She moved onto her side, her warm, naked skin rubbing against my thigh. I turned over, hugging her close until my rigid cock was pressed against the seam of her ass. Minx that she was, she wiggled against me, coaxing me to pin her down and do all the things I'd done to her last night over and over again.

"There is no other service. The minister is probably already with his family for the day."

"What, to go and ask for confession or something?" She yawned and snuggled against my chest.

"Catholics have confession. Not Baptists."

She shrugged. "Potato, tomato."

"Not the saying. Now, come on." I flipped the covers from over her and she yanked them back up again—although not before I caught sight of her creamy skin and full breasts.

"What? I'm not going anywhere. It's sleepy time."

She pulled the covers over her head, and I walked around to her side of the bed, kissing the lump on the comforter where I knew her head was hidden.

"We missed the service, but we still have Sunday lunch with Molly and Duke. If we don't show up, they'll come to check on us. And do you want them finding you like this?"

Her blue eyes peeked out from the edge of the comforter. "Maybe." She reached out from beneath it and ran a finger up the length of my thigh, tempting me from my knee to the inside of my leg, and then higher . . .

My cock gave a gratified twitch, and for a moment I pictured her leaning forward to take me in her mouth again, her morning hair still tousled as she moved her head up and down and worked me over.

"You like me," she teased, smiling as my cock twitched at the mental image.

I stepped away from her and pointed to where she'd left her suitcase.

"Come on and get dressed. We can talk about how much I like you later."

I headed for my dresser before I could see her pout—another reminder of how full and luscious those lips of hers were—and made quick work of dressing. Pulling my old Stallions ball cap over my head a few minutes later, I turned and found her all dolled up in a pretty lavender sundress that showed off her slender curves.

"You look incredible."

She grinned at me and I took her hand, ready to pull her to the truck, but before I did, she quickly lifted the hem of her dress, flashing me.

I blinked in surprise, my brain stuttering to a dead

stop. "Are you . . ."

She shook her head. "Nope. Not wearing panties. You know, in case you change your mind on the way there."

Hot. Damn. This woman would be the death of me.

Throwing her onto the bed, I decided it would be best to take a little detour before hitting the road.

• • •

Half an hour later, when we were both sated and her hair was more mussed than before, we jumped into the truck and hightailed it to What the Cluck. Duke's pickup was already in the parking lot, and we pulled up beside it.

Molly and Duke were waiting for us inside, the table already laden with our regular order of fried chicken, green beans, and biscuits. When I walked through the door, my sister gave me the kind of knowing look that made my cheeks warm.

If she'd been there, she would have known there was nothing I could do, though. Not when I had Charlotte so close and willing, sans panties.

Not when our time was almost up.

At least we'd shown up for lunch despite what we could be doing. Church was important, but family was my religion.

Charlotte and I sat on the bench opposite my siblings, and Molly grinned at us before offering us the plates she'd already dished out for us.

"How was church?" Charlotte asked brightly.

"It was wonderful. The sermon was about forgiveness," Molly said, eyeing me.

"Then you won't mind that we're late," I shot back, and Molly shot me another cutting look.

Duke just laughed. "We might, but I don't think Mr. and Mrs. French will." He nodded toward the older couple sitting in the corner of the room with the reverend and his wife.

"My absence was noted?" I raised my eyebrows.

Duke shrugged. "You know how Mrs. French is."

"I don't," Charlotte said, and I winced, wishing my

brother would stuff a sock in it.

"Mr. and Mrs. French feel strongly that their granddaughter needs to marry a nice boy from a good family," Duke explained.

"And since everyone knows Duke isn't the marrying type—" Molly added.

"Hey, hey, hey." Duke held up his hands. "I tried, if you recall."

"With Dana French?" Molly rolled her eyes. "Good move. No chance in hell."

"Why not?" Charlotte asked.

"She's more Luke's type," Duke said, and when Charlotte raised her eyebrows, Molly rushed in to explain.

"The Frenches just want someone who isn't going to leave Shady Grove. They're very close with Dana, especially now that her father passed."

"I see." Charlotte nodded. "And what do you think of Dana?" she asked me.

I glanced from my brother to my sister, not sure who

was more deserving of my glare. "I hardly know her."

"Unless you count every year of school from kindergarten to senior year of high school," Duke said.

"That doesn't mean I know her," I insisted. "She was in my classes, but I can't say I ever really talked to her."

Charlotte laughed. "It's okay, Luke. This isn't a trial. Is Dana pretty?"

I frowned. Why did Charlotte even want to hear about what I thought of another woman? She was leaving and this was all temporary, but on the other hand—

She'd shared my bed with me. Had been with me under the bleachers. Shouldn't some deeper, animal part of her be somewhat jealous? I tried to imagine myself in her shoes, and realized the thought of another guy touching her made me want to punch a hole through the fucking wall.

When I told Charlotte, "Not as pretty as you," she turned her attention to her chicken, eating with even more gusto than she had with her pretzel after the football game.

"Might have to order seconds if you're going to wolf it down like that," Duke teased, and she grinned.

"They don't make it like this where I'm from. So good. I'm trying to preserve the memory of the way this tastes." In a flash, she whipped out her phone and took a picture of the half-empty plate, complete with the orange-and-white What the Cluck wax paper underneath.

"Hashtag too good not to eat," she murmured to herself as she scrolled through the filters.

I laughed, then took a bite of my own chicken just in time for it to turn to dirt in my mouth as I looked up to find Wayne was walking toward us, his hands laden with carryout bags. He stopped at our table and grinned down at Charlotte.

"Oh. Hey, Wayne," she said with a polite half smile.

"Hey." He lifted the bags a little. "I was gonna call you, wanted to let you know your car should be all set around noon tomorrow. Whenever you're ready to pick it up after, you'll be good to go."

I studied her face, but it remained impassive as she nodded.

"Okay, great. Thanks again for your help."

When Wayne winked and headed for the door, I pushed my plate away, suddenly not hungry anymore. I knew there was an expiration date on my time with Charlotte—I'd reminded myself of that more times than I could count. But now that I knew the real timeline . . . now that I knew tonight was definitely our last night together?

It all felt different.

Wrong, somehow.

A combination of dread, doom, and despair mingled in my stomach. I looked up to catch Duke and Molly exchanging concerned glances, so this fact wasn't lost on them, but Charlotte continued to pick away at her food, seemingly oblivious.

Was it just me? Didn't she feel it too?

The thought that this strange sense of grief was one-sided made my temples throb.

"I guess your going-away party is going to have to be tonight then," Molly said.

Charlotte laughed. "Going away party? I've only been here a week."

"And every day has been better than the last. Come on, you can't say no." Molly grabbed a biscuit and took a big bite.

"Then I won't." Charlotte grinned from Molly to me, and I feigned a smile in return. "After all, it could be fun."

"Absolutely," I agreed with a little too much gusto. "Could be the best night of our lives."

That seemed about right. Sort of like the way a death row inmate's last meal was the most delicious one.

Chapter Sixteen

Charlotte

A couple of hours later, Luke and I splashed hand in hand through an unexpected rain shower and made it inside the bar just in time to see that when Molly said "party," she was so not kidding.

A buffet was set up in the corner of the room, and the honky-tonk's normal fluorescent lights had been dimmed to make way for the flashing Technicolor disco ball now hanging from the ceiling. She and Duke were sitting in the corner of the room, waiting for us, it seemed.

Everyone I'd seen or met in Shady Grove was crowded around the bar, and even a few people I hadn't met yet were dancing or clustered around the tables, talking to one another.

Luke and I laughed as Duke pretended to be affronted at our late arrival, and then I let out a low whistle as I took in the room again.

"How did you manage it? This must be the whole town," I said in amazement.

Molly laughed. "Just about. People around these parts love a party. Even Dana French is here," she said with a wink.

"Don't I know it." Duke grimaced at his brother. "Mrs. French thought I was you and tried to get me to dance with her."

I followed his gaze until I caught sight of the girl who had to be Dana. She was pretty and petite, with a sprinkle of freckles over her long, thin nose. Down her back, she wore a thick brown plait that was tied with a bright red ponytail holder.

"Classy," I said. "Her ponytail matches her dress." I knew I sounded bitchy, but damned if I could help it. She was adorable, and I hated her on sight.

That's a lie. I'd hated her from the second they'd mentioned her at the chicken place. It was petty and small and silly, but there it was.

Molly smirked. "Someone's jealous."

"As if." I rolled my eyes, but I turned so Molly couldn't see the nausea on my face. This party was super nice of her to do for me, and I wasn't about to be an ungrateful brat for any reason.

I made my way onto the dance floor and giggled with Molly until Luke appeared at my side, a drink in hand.

I raised my eyebrows. "What's up, cowboy?"

"I thought we should toast. I followed your advice."

I stopped dancing and looked up at him as Molly wandered away when a friend called her over. Luke's green eyes blazed with a proud light I'd never seen there before.

"What's up?" I asked.

"I followed your advice and struck a deal with Amos, the owner of the bar. Wilder is now their craft whiskey, and we worked together to come up with a signature cocktail. I want you to taste it."

When he held the glass out to me again, I took it and sipped slowly, then held my hand to my lips. It was beyond delicious—sweet and mild in all the best ways, but also dark and smoky without being too heavy. There was a hint of fruit and a splash of something that coated the back of my throat with a slow, silky burn, which made me want more.

"Oh my God," I murmured. "Did you come up with this?"

He nodded.

"What's in it?"

"If I tell you, I'd have to kill you," he said with a wink, and I rolled my eyes. "But it's sort of like a blackberry old-fashioned. A mix of something new and slick, and something classic and traditional."

When he gave me a meaningful look, I took another sip, savoring the sweet burn of the whiskey. "I've never had anything better."

For once, I wasn't sure if I was still talking about the whiskey or if it was something more, if it was all about this week here with him and these people who surrounded me. The people who cared so deeply about the Wilders that they'd gathered for a person they barely knew, just because it meant something to their neighbor.

There was a lot to be said about small towns, and that was one of them. Maybe Luke was constantly being set up with women. Maybe everyone knew everyone else's business. But they were there for each other. If something happened or someone did something special, there was never a lack of people there who wanted to help or to celebrate.

I thought of my phone that had only rung once more in the past couple of days, and even that call had been from a doctor I didn't know. Melancholy swept through me at that depressing thought.

Luke nodded toward my glass. "We're calling the drink a Little Wilder."

I smiled at him, pushing aside my sadness. This was an amazing day for him, and I couldn't be happier to be part of it. "Perfect. Absolutely perfect."

I took another swig and then passed the glass for him to share, but he downed it in one swallow and held out his hand for me. When I took it, he dragged me onto the dance floor just as the music slowed and began a deep, slow lullaby.

Being in Luke's arms, I let myself melt into him. When Wayne had stopped by the restaurant earlier, I'd been filled with such a sense of dread that I had to force my attention on my plate so Luke wouldn't see how wrecked I was. He didn't say a thing.

He spun me once, twice, then pulled me close, whispering against my hair. "It's been one hell of a week, duchess. I'll be sorry to see you go."

"Then don't."

I wasn't sure what made me say it, but Luke stilled and pulled back, his hand cupped under my chin.

"Ask me to stay," I whispered.

I'd never meant anything more in my life, but Luke looked at me like I'd just called him a filthy word.

"I thought you didn't need a man telling you what to do."

Confused, I stared at him, not sure what he was talking about. It took a moment for the memory to resurface, and when it did, it stung me as keenly as if he'd slapped me across the face.

"What? You're too proud to ask me?" I asked.

"I shouldn't have to. Come on, duchess, be reasonable."

"Be reasonable?" I blinked, suddenly aware that the burn in the back of my throat wasn't whiskey anymore, but the first sign of a wave of tears.

"I'm not asking you to stay. You should stay only if you want to."

He said it so matter-of-factly that I blinked again, waiting for the rest of his explanation, but it didn't come. Instead, he just stared at me.

Stunned, I nodded slowly. "Roger that."

I stepped away from him and slipped away through the crowd, glancing briefly toward Duke and Molly to make sure they were too preoccupied to notice when I slipped out the door and into the evening air.

So Luke didn't want me to stay? Fine. That was perfect. Or maybe he was just too stubborn to ask me. Either way, it didn't matter. I wasn't going to uproot my whole life for a man who couldn't mutter a few simple words. I deserved more than that.

Lightning cracked, followed by a slow rumble of thunder, and I lifted my face to the rain in hopes that it would hide my tears.

I'd stupidly put myself on the line and been shot down. Swallowing a sob, I glanced back at the bar before I broke into a jog, thankful I'd worn my flats.

Come tomorrow afternoon, I'd be long, long gone.

And apparently? That was the way Luke wanted it.

Chapter Seventeen

Luke

When I got home a little while later, the house was dark and empty, filled with nothing but the sound of rain tapping against the windowsill and the occasional rumble of thunder tearing through the hot Texas night.

To be honest, I wasn't sure what I'd expected. Maybe that Charlotte had waited for me the entire hour since she'd left, a reading light perched over her head in my living room as she pretended to read but stared at the front door.

I laughed at myself for even thinking such a stupid thought. Of course, she hadn't done that. A girl like Charlotte wasn't the type to sit around and wait for a guy, even if I'd asked her to.

She was like Sarah—she'd take action, do what she needed to in order to survive.

And this time? Apparently, that meant packing up her shit and getting the hell out of my house before I could even walk through the door to try to stop her. Which, of course, I also couldn't blame her for.

Fuck, I would have gotten the hell out of Dodge if I were her too. But, damn it, why did I always have to be the one to beg? Why couldn't she stay just because she wanted to?

With a deep breath, I made for the small makeshift bar in the corner of the living room. There I grabbed the newest bottle of whiskey and poured myself a glass.

It had been raining the night Sarah left too, though that had been a flash of summer rain. Tonight was different. It was wild and torrential, fat droplets spattering the dusty ground and turning it into a mud slick.

Had it rained the morning our mother had left?

It felt like it was possible.

I swigged my whiskey, then thought again of the look on Charlotte's face when she'd tasted the drink I'd concocted. It was like she'd lit up, so bright and animated. When was the last time I'd seen a face like that—of someone who believed in me so much? Someone who wasn't Duke or Molly?

That certainly hadn't been Sarah's expression when I'd told her about going back to the distillery.

"Your father? What the hell has he ever done for you? You need to stop worrying about all that and focus on us."

Sarah had believed in her dream, but not mine. And in the end, wasn't that what had made her go? And with Mom, wasn't it her not believing in Dad that had made her leave?

Logically, their choices had nothing to do with me or my dad. But how it felt . . .

How it felt had nothing to do with logic.

I took another pull from my glass and sat it on a stool before closing my eyes and pinching the bridge of my nose. Again, with my eyes closed to the world, I saw nothing but Charlotte beaming back at me, holding the drink she'd been the inspiration for, even if she didn't know it.

Could I really throw all that away? Could I let her get into her car tomorrow and drive out of my life forever without even telling her how I felt?

I took another sip and shook my head as I was surrounded by sudden and complete darkness. A flash of light filled the air as lightning cracked again, followed quickly by a slap of thunder.

"Damn power outage," I mumbled, but then I thought of Charlotte alone in her room at the inn, probably sitting in darkness without any candles.

I ought to go check on her.

I wouldn't ask her to stay. How could I? Even though she believed in me and I cared for her, I'd only known her for a week. But I could tell her how much I wished it could be different. And I could tell her how much I'd enjoyed her company. And then maybe she'd decide she wanted to stay.

What I knew for sure was that I couldn't let things end like this.

Grabbing a few of the emergency candles I kept in my foyer closet, I headed for the truck and made quick work of driving through the onslaught of rain. The inn wasn't far from my place, and before I knew it, I was parked in front of the familiar Victorian house as it was lit up by another flash of lightning.

Quickly, I snatched up the candles and sprinted

inside, stopping only to ask Opal, the innkeeper, for Charlotte's new room number before I bounded upstairs. When I hammered on the door, I heard her squeak in surprise.

"Charlotte? It's me. Can I come in?"

"No," she murmured, her voice sounding husky and quiet.

"Come on. It has to be dark in there, and I brought candles. Just let me know you're okay."

The door swung open and Charlotte's face appeared, lit by the soft glow of a candle she held below her face. "Opal gave me one when the power went out. Honestly, how helpless do you think I am?"

I opened my mouth and then closed it.

"Look," Charlotte blurted, "you made yourself perfectly clear. You don't want me to stay and that's okay, but I don't really want to beat this to death, you know? I feel kind of stupid for even mentioning it, and—"

"Don't. Please don't feel stupid. I had an amazing time with you. It's just—"

I craned my neck, acutely aware that Opal hadn't made a peep in all the time we'd been talking, but was clearly able to hear us from down the hall. I'd bet money she was poised at the foot of the stairs, listening.

"Can you let me in so we can talk privately?"

Charlotte blew out a breath and stepped aside to allow me in. By the light of her candle, I could see that her eyes were gleaming with tears, and I felt like a total shit.

I paced the floor, then put the candles on the dresser before turning to face her. "Look, I'm not going to ask you to stay. I made that mistake before and it didn't work out so well for me, but it also could've worked out way worse. Even if it had been okay with you and me at first, eventually you would've wound up resenting me, and we'd have ended up hating each other."

"So now I'm Sarah?" Charlotte's voice raised an octave, and I cringed.

"No, that's not what I'm saying. It's just . . . I've only known you a week, and we both know you don't belong here." I hated even thinking it, but saying it out loud, I knew it was true.

"What the hell is that supposed to mean?" she demanded.

"It's not an insult." I held up my hands. "You're beautiful and cultured, and yes, you may think you want to stay here with a guy that you've only known for a week. But when time goes on and you realize that you're sick of fried chicken and you can't stand that there's not a decent theater or shopping mall anywhere nearby? Shady Grove isn't going to be enough for you."

"That's not true." Her voice dropped to a whisper. "You don't know that. You don't know *me* if you think that's all I care about."

"Maybe I don't. But don't you think that could be a problem too?"

She sucked in a deep breath and stared at me. Even in the candlelight, I could see the tears slipping from her eyes, finally breaking free. My heart gave a squeeze, and I resisted the urge to yank her close to me and take it all back.

"You're right, okay? Is that what you want me to say? Wanting to stay here is a pipe dream." She took a step closer to me, her bottom lip trembling. "It was just so good between us, Luke. What if we never find that again with anyone else?"

The very thought of her with anyone else made my gut tense. The thought of her in another man's arms made me want to hit something.

Don't think about it, man.

"So I can't stay," she added. "But does that mean we have to spend this last night apart?"

Jesus. Even after I'd hurt her, she wanted to be with me one last time, and it was what I wanted more than anything too. To hold her in my arms and take her, to claim her as my own. We would fit together so perfectly—like two missing puzzle pieces—and I would feel even worse when I had to watch her drive away from me in the morning.

But if I said no to her again? I knew I'd regret it for the rest of my life. And I had enough regrets.

I walked toward her and tucked my hand under her chin, pulling her lips to mine until I could taste the minty-sweet toothpaste on her tongue and the oaky, rich flavor of honeyed whiskey on her breath. The perfect combination. The perfect girl.

Before I knew it, we were falling backward onto the bed until she let out a soft sigh and connected with the mattress.

"Luke."

When she breathed my name, I kissed her again, tucking her hair behind her ear as my tongue searched deeper inside her mouth, pulling her toward me, claiming her with my lips.

"Come home with me," I whispered, and she nodded, her head tucked under my chin.

A few minutes later, we ran for the truck, rain pelting us sideways as she left without taking a thing. Once we were back at my place, I led her to my bedroom, each of us carrying a lit candle to guide our path.

Stripping down to my boxers, I watched as Charlotte shed her wet clothes. After dressing her in one of my T-shirts, I led her to my bed.

I kissed her lips softly in a moment so sweet and

perfect, it almost didn't seem real. It felt like something out of one of those cheesy Nicholas Sparks movies that Molly liked. The raindrops pelting the windows, the sound of Charlotte's shallow breaths, the way her lips met mine . . . I wasn't a romantic, but the knot in my throat and the ache in my chest felt very real.

I wouldn't make love to her tonight. I knew if I claimed her again, I'd never let go.

Come morning, it would be agony to watch her leave, but at least I'd still have my pride. I wouldn't have begged or pleaded. She wouldn't wake up and hate me one day for asking. And I'd be able to go on knowing we'd both been happy for a time, which was all we'd ever wanted from the arrangement.

I didn't tell her that, though. Instead, I pulled away from the kiss despite everything inside me urging me on, and held her tight.

"You okay?" I whispered.

"I am now."

We curled together in the darkness, sharing pieces of our pasts. Charlotte spoke again about her overbearing parents and wanting to make a decision that was just hers, while I shared my dreams of making my whiskey a household name. I told her stories of my mom and dad, and growing up in a small town. She talked about the lingering ideas she still had for the distillery, promising to call if she came up with any more, but I secretly hoped she wouldn't.

Because if I heard her voice again?

I'd crack faster than a priest at a Vegas strip club.

Chapter Eighteen

Luke

I rose from bed early the next morning, unable to sleep with the knowledge that today was the day. Creeping into the bathroom while Charlotte slept, I turned on the shower and waited for the water to warm.

As I soaped up, I reflected on everything that had happened. This past week had been one of the best of my life. I didn't know it, but before Charlotte arrived, I'd been living in a fog. I'd wake up early, work all day, stress the fuck out over the distillery turning a profit one of these days, then fall into bed exhausted. But ever since she showed up here, my miserable little routine had been interrupted in the best way imaginable.

Watching Charlotte blossom and grow during her stay here had been something, and I wanted to believe that I'd had a hand in that. Gone was the uptight, spoiled rich girl who expected everything to be done at the snap of her fingers. In her place was a beautiful, confident woman who was learning to roll with the punches and make lemon drops from lemons.

After rinsing off, I grabbed a towel and wrapped it around my waist. Swiping at the fog in the mirror, I scowled at the reflection staring back at me.

What the fuck am I supposed to do?

Running a hand across my jaw, I decided that forgoing shaving today wouldn't be the worst thing in the world. Charlotte liked my scruff. The thought made me crack a smile.

But then it hit me again that she wouldn't be here later to stroke her fingers along my jaw and tell me that she loved me like this. That thought stung.

Padding back into my bedroom wearing just a towel, I grabbed a pair of jeans and a T-shirt, dressing quietly before Charlotte woke.

Curled onto her side with a spray of dark hair spread across the pillow, she looked so soft and sweet in her sleep. Smirking, I realized that the woman was anything but soft. Awake, she was a feisty firecracker who never hesitated to put me in my place.

As if sensing my presence, Charlotte turned toward

me, blinking against the sunlight streaming in through the blinds.

"Morning, sleepyhead."

"What time is it?" she asked.

"Just after eight."

Sitting up, she grabbed her phone and deleted a couple of text messages without bothering to read them. Probably just her friend in LA giving her a hard time about her lengthy stopover. Charlotte and I both knew that Wayne could have been pressured into having her car done sooner.

"You hungry?" I asked.

"Can I shower first?"

I nodded. "Take your time."

That statement was all wrong. Time was the one thing we didn't have. But Charlotte brushed her tangled hair away from her face and smiled weakly at me. That sad little smile tore through me like a knife.

"I'll be downstairs," I murmured, heading for the

door. I found Duke in the kitchen fixing himself a plate of eggs.

"What's on the agenda today?" he asked.

I cleared my throat, forcing down the knot that had formed. "Charlotte's taking off today."

"And that's it, huh?"

"Yeah. Guess so."

He slammed the skillet he'd just washed onto the counter. "Don't be a dumb fuck. She's perfect for you."

He was wrong about that. She was way too good for someone like me, and I wouldn't trap her into something she'd regret.

"I won't ask her to stay."

He shook his head. "Then show her why leaving would be stupid."

Tingles started at the base of my spine as a plan formed in my mind. I needed to make a call, and my cell was still in my bedroom.

"Give me your phone," I demanded.

Duke gave me that cocky crooked grin he always wore when he'd just outsmarted me, and handed me his phone.

Glancing toward the stairs to make sure there was no sight of Charlotte, I dialed the number for Wayne's. Several rings later, I was almost convinced his lazy ass wasn't even up yet when he finally answered.

"Yup," he said.

"Wayne. It's Luke Wilder."

"What can I do for ya?"

"I've got a crisp hundred-dollar bill with your name on it if you can keep the Audi in the shop today."

He was quiet, and I had the sinking feeling he was going to refuse to play along. Duke nodded, watching me.

"I just need one more day," I said.

"All right then. I'll see you tomorrow," Wayne said and then clicked off.

A little while later, Charlotte came downstairs, her

skin freshly scrubbed and dewy, and her damp hair hanging down her back.

"Wayne called to say things didn't go according to plan, and he said to come by tomorrow morning." She shrugged and took a seat at the breakfast table, but she didn't seem particularly upset.

Duke smiled at me and took his plate of eggs to the other room, giving us some privacy.

Today was my last chance to show her everything our life could be if she'd only take a chance. I couldn't waste this opportunity. Maybe, just maybe, if I played my cards right, she'd make the decision to stay all on her own.

"First, I'm going to feed you," I said, setting down a mug of steaming coffee in front of Charlotte.

"And then what?"

"I think we can entertain ourselves for one more day, don't you?"

• • •

After breakfast, Charlotte took my truck into town to check out of the inn and get her suitcase. While she was gone, I got to work, packing up a picnic basket while Molly supervised with a grin.

So far, I had cheese, crackers, fruit, hot dogs and buns, and a bottle of white wine. Molly was getting a little too much joy out of this, but without her help, the basket would have probably only contained a bottle of whiskey and a whole bunch of condoms.

After adding a couple of red plastic cups from the pantry, I surveyed my work. *Not bad.*

"Pass me those napkins," I told Molly.

"Here, take these instead." She handed me two cloth napkins, and then switched out my plastic cups for a pair of stemless wineglasses.

While I grabbed a blanket from the hall closet, Molly darted off, then emerged from her bedroom with a little package of salted caramel dark chocolate squares.

"These are your favorite," I said. "Are you sure?"

She nodded. "Charlotte loves them too."

I added those to the basket, along with graham crackers and a bag of marshmallows.

"Where are you taking her?" Molly asked.

"I'm thinking the swimming hole, a picnic, maybe a bonfire and a movie on the iPad if she likes the idea."

Molly's gaze went soft. "How sweet. It'll be like your own private outdoor movie."

"Yep. That's the idea." Privacy was my main goal, that and showing her all the pleasures life in a small town had to offer.

"Oh!" Molly ran to the hall closet. "You're gonna need some pillows. Maybe a couple more blankets too."

Tires crunching on gravel out front meant Charlotte was back, and I turned to Molly and handed her the blanket.

"Throw the pillows and blankets in the back of the truck for me, would you?"

Molly nodded and hurried toward the screen door.

I snatched up the basket and on second thought,

grabbed the whiskey and condoms, tucking those in too. After all, a man could never be too prepared.

"What's all this for?" Charlotte asked as she climbed out of the truck and handed me the keys.

I placed the basket behind the seat. "Just get your pretty little ass back in the truck, and you'll see." I swatted her behind playfully while Molly waved from the front porch.

"Yes, sir," Charlotte muttered under her breath.

She fiddled with the radio until she found a station that suited her while I headed out toward the spot I had in mind. What we needed was privacy, and I knew just the place. About a half hour outside of town on a stretch of country road was a piece of land I'd looked at buying last year. Acres of rolling hills and shady pecan trees, and a rocky bluff overlooking the clearest, prettiest lake. It was completely secluded with no one for miles around.

The owner, an old man in his eighties, wasn't ready to sell, but told me I was free to visit whenever I wanted to go fishing in the lake. I had a lot more on my mind today than catching a few catfish.

"Where are we headed?" Charlotte asked. "Am I dressed okay?"

Looking down at her delicious creamy thighs below a pair of cut-off jean shorts—thighs that I hoped would be wrapped around my neck later—I just grinned. "You're perfect."

A little while later, we pulled down the hidden single-lane road that was so narrow, twigs and branches brushed the sides of my truck as we drove on.

Charlotte gave me a worried look. "Will you tell me where you're taking me? Because this is looking more and more like somewhere you go to get rid of a body."

Chuckling at her, I finally pulled to a stop in a clearing overlooking the lake. "I figured I had one last day to show you all the pleasures of the simple life, and I didn't want to waste it."

She gazed out the windshield to the lake beyond, and as hard as I tried to decipher her expression, I couldn't quite read it.

This was my last shot, and I was pulling out all the

stops.

Chapter Nineteen

Charlotte

The asshat had conveniently forgotten to mention that I needed a bathing suit. But I couldn't be mad because getting to see Luke, a whole lot of Luke, all tanned skin and rock-hard muscle, made it totally worth it. Plus, I'd never been skinny-dipping, so I got to cross that off my bucket list.

We played in the shallows for a while, and then he carried me out into deeper water and kissed me. He became aroused, and for a moment I thought we might make love right there in the lake, but we didn't. Instead, he dunked me and swam away laughing, which spawned a twenty-minute water battle.

Then we dressed and grabbed what Luke had brought. He led me on a hike around the lake, finally climbing up to a rocky bluff where we could see for miles. We spread out the blanket on a perfect spot and cuddled together, watching the clouds float by. It was truly the perfect day already, and it was barely even noon.

"You getting hungry yet?" Luke asked, leaning over

to brush a wisp of hair away from my face.

"Maybe. What's in that picnic basket?"

Smirking, he said, "You'll just have to find out."

We sat up, stacking up the oversized throw pillows behind us, and Luke arranged an impressive picnic. We munched on cheese and crackers, and sipped glasses of wine while chatting about everything and nothing.

"This is an awfully romantic date, Mr. Wilder. Explain to me again how it is that you're still single?"

He chuckled and shook his head. "No, you've got it all wrong. This isn't a date. I just needed to get you out of the house before the hookers that Duke hired came over."

Knowing he was kidding, I nodded, keeping my expression serious. "I see. Good plan."

He told me about the history of Shady Grove, and how his family came to be settled there. We laughed and ate, and then watched a movie on the iPad he'd brought. It was the perfect day.

When the sun began to set, I thought that was it, that it was time to pack up and go home. Instead, Luke went to gather firewood while I built a little stone ring several feet away from our blanket. Once he got a fire going, we roasted hot dogs on sticks and ate gooey burned marshmallows, chasing them with sips of his smoky whiskey.

I couldn't recall a time when I'd enjoyed such simple pleasures. As sweet as it had been for Molly to throw me a going-away party, *this* was the best way to spend my last night here. It felt so right.

"You cold?" Luke asked, draping a heavy arm around me and pulling me close.

"A little." I nodded.

"I'll fix that."

After he threw another log onto the fire, he stood up and grabbed a faded flannel shirt from his truck, then draped it around my shoulders. The shirt was soft and smelled like him, and I slipped my arms into the sleeves and buttoned it up.

"I'm a mess," I said, smoothing my wavy air-dried hair into a ponytail high on my head. I could only imagine what I must look like.

"I like you like this," Luke murmured, tilting my chin toward his to kiss my lips.

"You're being awfully sweet. Are you trying to get lucky?" I whispered, pressing my lips to his again.

"That depends . . ."

"On?"

Luke lifted me into his lap, settling me over the firm ridge in his pants. "On if you can handle riding this all night long." He thrust upward, forcing the breath from my lungs. "Because I don't plan on stopping until the sun comes up."

His mouth crashed against mine in a hungry kiss. The pressure building between my legs demanded attention, and I couldn't help the whimper that fell from my lips.

He groaned when I shifted my hips, gripping my ass to work me over his straining cock as he kissed me again. After unbuttoning the flannel shirt, Luke let it drop from my shoulders and then stripped off my T-shirt and bra.

His warm, calloused palms covered my breasts, his

thumbs stroking my nipples. "What do you say, sweetheart? Are you ready to ride my cock?"

Rising to my feet, I quickly stripped out of my shorts and underwear. Luke wasted no time unfastening his pants and shoving them down his hips. By the time I was back in his lap, he'd already sheathed himself in a condom.

"Come here, beautiful. Need to make sure you're ready for me."

While his mouth feasted on my breasts—kissing and nibbling and licking—his hand moved between us where he discovered that I was, in fact, already ready for him.

"I love it when you taste like my whiskey." He groaned again, sliding one finger inside me.

Gripping his shoulders, I buried my face against his neck, kissing all the warm skin I could reach. "Luke . . ." I moaned his name, the need in my voice unmistakable.

Positioning me in his lap, he pressed forward slowly until our bodies were joined.

"Christ . . . you're perfect," he said, grunting as he

pumped into me.

"Let me," I whispered.

Placing his hands on my jaw, he brought my lips to his while I took control of our speed. I rocked my hips in his lap, finding the angle that suited me.

I patted his chest. "Lean back, big boy."

Luke obeyed, resting on his elbows while he watched me with hooded eyes. "Just like that, baby. Nice and slow."

Under the moon and stars with a fire crackling beside us, we found new ways to bring each other pleasure. And after we had both reached our climax, we lay spooned together under a blanket for a long time, his breathing slow and even as he stroked my hair.

I kept waiting for Luke to ask me to stay, waited for him to ask what was so important about getting to LA.

But he didn't.

And I didn't bring it up, even though I felt the weight of my secret pressing down on me with each passing heartbeat. Because now that we'd grown closer, keeping the truth from him this whole time suddenly felt very, very wrong.

"Luke, there's something I never told you about back home . . . about why I left."

"Shh." He stroked my hair. "You don't owe me an explanation. You wanted a fresh start, right?"

I nodded, my head still nestled against his chest. Tears welled in my eyes at how perfect and sweet this man was. He'd bared his soul to me in just one week's time, and I hadn't even been brave enough to return the favor. But for now, I knew he was right. I didn't want to sully our last night together by talking about Prescott or any of the other stuff in my life. Compared to the man beside me, it was all meaningless.

Tomorrow had the power to change everything, so I kept my mouth shut and simply enjoyed being with him.

But I couldn't help but wonder, come morning, would he ask me to stay, or would he let me go without a fight?

Chapter Twenty

Luke

Last night had been perfect. Charlotte and I had lain together under the stars until the moon was high, but when the temperature started to drop, we packed up for home, making love once more in my bed.

The day had been filled with sunshine and laughs and the hottest sex of my life, but in the end, it hadn't really changed anything. Charlotte didn't mention the future, and though I wondered where her head was at, I didn't have the balls to bring it up.

If I had, I knew I'd probably end up begging her to stay, and I'd only come to regret it. Just like I had with my mom, and just like I had with Sarah. There were sayings about this exact situation—about being burned, or fool me once, shit like that—and I didn't care to see history repeat itself.

Charlotte rose early, and I made coffee while she showered. When she was dressed, she came downstairs with her suitcase, her expression unreadable. She hugged Molly good-bye one last time while my sister shot me a questioning scowl.

Leave it, my expression said.

"Ready?" I asked after they exchanged phone numbers and promised to stay in touch.

Charlotte nodded.

I tossed her suitcase in the back of my truck and we got in, the silence hanging around us nearly deafening.

Without a word, Duke got in his truck to follow us over to Wayne's. He knew without my saying that if she got in that car today, I'd be gutted. He also knew I'd head over to the bar and drink until I couldn't walk anymore. He'd be there to drive me home, and later, to help me pick up the pieces.

When we pulled up, her shiny black Audi was parked out front. As we climbed out of my truck, Wayne came strolling out of the shop, and an impending sense of doom settled over me.

This was it.

Chapter Twenty-One

Charlotte

We pulled to a stop in the same dusty gravel driveway I'd broken down in ten days ago. It was crazy how fast my life had changed since meeting Luke. It was crazy how deeply he, his family, and this little town had affected me.

I followed Wayne inside the shop to settle my bill and collect my key while Luke and his brother exchanged some tense words in the parking lot. I didn't know why Duke was here, maybe just to say good-bye one last time, but it felt like something more than that. I tried not to think about it.

After giving my parents' black credit card a healthy workout, there was no other reason to delay. Inhaling one last deep breath of fresh country air as I walked through the parking lot, I realized this was it.

While Duke helped me load my suitcase into the trunk of the car, Wayne and Luke stood and talked at the edge of the parking lot.

I could barely stand to look at Luke—it hurt too much. The thought that I might be speaking my last words to him cut me to the core. Yesterday had been incredible, probably the best day of my entire life, but that was all it was. One last day to enjoy each other before it all came to an end because he hadn't asked me to stay, and I certainly wasn't going to invite myself to.

If he really wanted me here, he would have made that clear. Luke wasn't a man who minced words.

"You sure you have to go, sweetheart?" Duke asked, drawing me out of my thoughts.

I closed the trunk and turned to face him. Anger and frustration were etched into his features, but I sensed all his anger was directed at his brother, not me.

I gave him a sad smile.

"He's an idiot to let you go," Duke said, taking my hand and giving it a squeeze. "If you won't stay for him, stay for me."

His sensitivity touched me. I'd never seen the softer, more serious side of Duke, but it was obvious there was one.

"It's not that simple," I said.

"Why not?"

Shielding my eyes from the sun, I took a deep breath, forcing from my throat the words I didn't want to say out loud. "First of all, he never asked me to stay."

"Fucking dipshit," Duke said under his breath. "You know he bribed Wayne, don't you? You could've gotten out of here yesterday."

That was news to me, but it felt like too little, too late. "Doesn't matter. We had fun, and now it's over."

Luke knew how I felt. I'd put my heart out there the night of my party, asked him to tell me to stay. He wouldn't, and now it was too late.

Chapter Twenty-Two

Luke

After handing Wayne his money, I watched as Duke said one last good-bye to Charlotte and then climbed into his truck. Wayne went back inside, and then it was just Charlotte and me.

"The end of the road," I murmured, and she nodded.

I didn't know what to say, and it seemed she didn't either. I folded her into my arms one last time, trying not to notice how perfectly she fit there. There were no tears, no long drawn-out good-bye, and no promises to keep in touch. She had stormed into my life, but it seemed she was leaving without the same flair.

I thought about kissing her good-bye, but in the end, I couldn't. I simply helped her into her car, shut the door, then watched as she drove off into the distance, my fists clenched at my sides and my stomach tight with despair.

But as that fancy foreign car disappeared over the horizon, I couldn't shake the feeling that it was taking my heart along with it.

Chapter Twenty-Three

Charlotte

I cried all the way through the rest of Texas, New Mexico, and Arizona. For three days, I drove toward LA, thinking over the past week in Shady Grove and trying to convince myself not to turn back.

I wanted to run into Luke's house and demand that he realize I wasn't the same as Sarah, that things would be different with me if he'd only give it a chance. But then, whenever I was leaving one highway motel or another, I would realize that my actions—no matter how grand— would do nothing to change his mind.

He was a traditionalist, down to the stereotype of being stuck in his ways, and if I thought I was going to be the one to change him? Well, I had another think coming.

No, Luke Wilder and everything he stood for was in the rearview now—just like New York and Prescott and all the rest of my past.

Suddenly, this move didn't feel like starting over or starting fresh anymore. It simply felt like . . . settling. As if every mile I got closer to LA, I was getting a little farther from what I actually wanted.

I was excited to see Valentina, of course, but even when I finally pulled up to my friend's house, it was with a growing sense of doom and despair.

After hauling my suitcase from the backseat, I trudged up the little stoop outside Valentina's chic bungalow and rang the doorbell. In an instant, my friend was there, all tanned willowy limbs and long dark curls, embracing me in a hug that seemed to go on forever.

Which, of course, only made the tears I thought I'd managed to leave behind in Arizona spring back up and rear their ugly heads.

"What's wrong, honey?" Valentina cooed as she ushered me inside.

I sniffled before following her, swiping away my tears with the back of my hand. "I'm sorry. I'm being stupid."

"You are many things, but stupid is not one of them." She gestured to her bright white couch and I took a seat carefully, wiping away another errant tear. "What's going on?"

I let the whole story spill out—or, at least, the parts of it she didn't already know. I was a little ashamed that I shared more than I probably should have. About the hot sex and the burning attraction between Luke and me. About what we'd said to each other in our intimate moments. About how he'd held me all night before I left, and the way he hadn't even kissed me good-bye.

About how he refused to ask me to stay.

Through it all, Valentina sat in rapt attention, nibbling at her long, perfectly manicured fingernails and nodding in all the right places. When I finally finished, she sat back and let out a wistful little sigh.

"Well, that sounds like it was all long overdue."

"What?" I asked.

"Think about the guys you've been with," she said with a shrug. "You needed someone outside your comfort zone. You needed to have a little brush with real love."

"But Prescott—"

She rolled her eyes. "Are you really going to sit here and tell me—me, your best friend since kindergarten—

that you were in love with Prescott?"

"I was going to marry him," I shot back.

"Which, I'll remind you, had nothing to do with love. Your parents just wanted to see that you didn't squander that tidy little inheritance of yours. He was well bred, just like you. For God's sake, that relationship was more like two animals mating in captivity than actually—"

I made a little choking noise and Valentina stopped short.

"What?" she asked.

"Well, I never actually . . . Prescott and I didn't . . ."

Valentina let out a disgusted snort. "You were going to marry a guy you'd never slept with? What is this, the eighteen hundreds?"

I closed my eyes. "Marrying him just seemed like the practical thing to do. We got along well and traveled in the same circles."

"God, that is the most depressing reason for getting married I've ever heard. I'm so glad you weren't going to write your own vows. You probably would have cited the tax codes that made marriage such a great decision." She rolled her eyes again, tsk-tsking at me. "Come on, we both know the real reason you were going to marry him, and it wasn't because he was practical and respectable."

I raised my eyebrows.

"Are you really going to make me say it out loud?" Valentina said, and I stared at her blankly.

As far as I knew, I'd gotten engaged to Prescott because he'd asked me, and because it made a certain kind of sense on paper. Anything other than that would have been news to me.

"You don't think you were just so desperate to please Mommy and Daddy that you were ready to commit yourself to their all-star team pick for your husband?"

I scoffed. "I don't know what you—"

"Charlotte, I saw you after your father turned you down for that job at his company. And I was there when your mother sniffed at your prom date and asked about his last name. I know what those people do to you. You're never good enough for them. But with Prescott, you had a chance to finally—"

"That's not true," I said, a sick feeling welling up inside me, but Valentina ignored me.

"Prescott had a better family name, a bigger inheritance, and a prettier penthouse than yours. No wonder Mommy and Daddy were so gung-ho about this union. Their social stock would climb like nobody's business."

I chewed on my bottom lip, not willing to give in yet. God, the person she was describing sounded so pathetic. Poor little rich girl, desperate for her parents to love her. That couldn't be me.

"My parents' approval is important to me, but it's not everything."

"And that's why you made the right decision and left." Valentina gave me an approving nod. "But tell me, when was the last time they really listened to what you thought or what you wanted? You can't go on like this, just living life to please them, and they need to know it."

She jerked her head toward the phone on the coffee

table between us. "Tomorrow, you call. But for now? You've had a long trip. I think you should take a nice hot shower, have a nap, and then we'll hit the town. Come morning, you can decide what to say to your parents. And Luke. Maybe even Prescott too."

"You're too wise for your own good," I said, and she laughed.

"I get that a lot."

So, that afternoon, I did as she suggested. I took a shower and then lay down to sleep, but whenever I closed my eyes, I felt like I was in Luke's bed, waiting for his warm, strong arm to wind its way around me and pull me close. Waiting for him to smell my hair and kiss the back of my neck. Wanting him to pull me close and whisper something dirty in my ear. Waiting for something that would never come again.

Of course, in the rare moments I didn't think about Luke, I considered my life. My choices.

I was, I knew, a daughter of privilege. I had no student loans and no debt to speak of, a fancy car I hadn't paid for myself, and a black credit card I could whip out at a moment's notice.

But at what cost?

My mother's indignation when I made a choice she didn't like. My father's continued disapproval. The expectation that I would continue in their footsteps by marrying well and raising children who would live sheltered, privileged lives just like mine, with a history of cold boarding schools and even chillier romances.

And the more I thought about it, the more I realized it wasn't a price I was willing to pay.

Chapter Twenty-Four

Luke

It had been three days since Charlotte had left, and in all that time I hadn't bothered to leave the barn.

Well, that wasn't entirely true. The day she left, Duke had taken me into town and I'd gotten shit-faced drunk. Then I spent the next day in bed, pretending to be hung over, but I was really just heartbroken.

Now, though? Now, I was determined. Throwing myself into my work seemed to be the best distraction I could find.

Our first public unveiling would take place in a month, and there was still so much to do, so many events to plan. My face was rough with unshaven stubble and my eyes were dark with exhaustion, but in the end, I knew it would be worth it. The barn would house more than just a distillery—it would be a hometown tasting room complete with special lighting and ambience, all the touches that Charlotte had so carefully laid out for us.

If only I didn't see her face . . . feel her touch . . . smell her hair every second of the day.

She'd come up with half the specialty mixes for the tasting bar, the ideas for the whiskey-barrel pub tables, and the burlap coasters with the branded design on them. Even as I strung the lights from the rafters, I could recall the way she'd laughed at me when I asked why it mattered so much that we got Edison bulbs instead of twinkling Christmas lights.

"See?" she'd said. "This is why you need me."

I ran my hand over my scraggly beard, then climbed down from the ladder and snapped a few shots. Soon, I'd be sending off my ideas to investors to see if we could expand the barn—make it into a full-scale grand destination. Something for parties and weddings.

That, I realized with a thud of my heart, had been Charlotte's idea too.

A light knock sounded against the door behind me, and I turned to find my sister leaning against the door frame.

"Wow." Molly let out a low whistle. "Duke said you'd been hard at work, but I never imagined . . ."

The place was pretty impressive. I'd built the tasting bar myself, and had already arranged four of the sixteen bar stools that would be clustered around the wide oak-barrel tables. A lantern sat in the center of each table, and as I flipped a switch, the soft light of the Edison bulbs overhead let me know that Charlotte had been right. The soft yellow glow made all the difference, especially on a rainy day like today.

"You like it?" I asked.

"I think it's perfect." Molly nodded. "Looks like you had help, though."

I cleared my throat, trying to sound casual. "Charlotte ordered most of it before she left. I just had to set the place up."

"If only she could see it now," Molly said with a pointed look. "I bet she wouldn't believe it's the same barn you showed her around before."

"Well, she did have a soft spot for the place."

"She'd be proud."

"Yeah, I bet she would."

Molly slid onto one of the stools in front of the tasting bar. "Hey, make me a Little Wilder, huh?"

I made quick work of mixing her drink, and when I passed it her way, she lifted the glass slightly.

"This one was your idea, right?"

I nodded. "Yeah."

"I can tell. Traditional old-fashioned with a little twist of something modern."

"Look, Molly—"

She held up a hand to silence me. "I'm not trying to influence you one way or another. Your life is your business," she said with a little sigh. "But if you ask for my opinion, on the other hand—"

"Which I haven't," I reminded her.

"Which you haven't, but if you did, I would tell you what I really thought." She took a sip of her drink and waited, knowing that I'd have to ask.

"Fine. What do you think?"

"I think you've been a miserable prick since Charlotte left, and you let her go for no good reason."

I let out a humorless laugh. "Is that all?"

"She hasn't posted even a single Instagram pic since we all when to What the Cluck. I'm thinking she's probably pretty miserable too."

"In Los Angeles? A girl like her? I doubt it," I said, although my selfish heart lifted at the thought that she might miss me. That even some small portion of her was hurting the way I'd been hurting—even though she couldn't possibly be as haunted by my absence as I was by hers.

"I think you were too quick to judge her," Molly said.

I shrugged. "You weren't with us all the time."

Molly sat down her drink with a *thunk* and waggled a finger at me. "I was with you enough, and I've been around you all your life. Don't think I don't know what you're doing. I saw what happened at the party."

"What do you—"

"I was in the corner talking to Dana French, and I

heard Charlotte tell you to ask her to stay."

My heart dropped into my stomach. "I asked for your opinion, not a recounting of the facts."

"Fine, then, here's my opinion. You're a dumbass."

"Molly—"

"You forget that I knew Sarah. I was going to be the maid of honor at your wedding. I was there when Dad . . ." Molly cleared her throat and gathered herself before she continued. "I was only around Charlotte for a week, but I'm here to tell you that while you do have a definite type, those two are most certainly *not* interchangeable people. Charlotte would never have left you like that, without a word right after Dad died. Sarah was self-involved and entitled. Charlotte isn't like that."

"How would you know?" I shot back.

"Look around this room," Molly said simply. "You didn't pay her for this. Charlotte helped you out of the goodness of her heart, and she never once told you to give up."

"That doesn't change the fact that she'd never be

happy in Shady Grove," I said, although my argument sounded feeble, even to me.

"You never know anything until you try. And you? You're afraid of trying." Molly shoved off her stool, then pulled the hood of her rain jacket over her head. "Look, I have a feeling that no matter what I say, you're going to have some argument for me, so I'm not going to waste my breath. I only came to tell you that a letter came today from an investor who saw your pictures online. He's coming to see the place next week."

A little thrill of excitement ran through me, but it did nothing to assuage the guilt and turmoil borne by everything Molly had said. What followed was a tiny grain of something like hope.

"Don't work yourself to death in here," Molly added, then hunched over and hurried out into the rain.

I glanced at her half-empty glass and then reached for my phone. Scrolling through my contacts, I opened Charlotte's information and stared at it, my thumb hovering over the CALL button for what felt like the hundredth time.

Logically, I knew it was better to cut things off with her cold turkey. But after everything, Molly had said . . .

I shoved the phone back in my pocket and headed for my truck, my head whirling with everything that needed to be done before the investor showed up. It also spun with all the reasons I shouldn't pull out my phone and see if Molly was right.

To see if Charlotte missed me.

Chapter Twenty-Five

On my second day at Valentina's, I summoned my courage and picked up my phone, finding another slew of missed calls and texts.

None, I noticed, were from Luke.

I was going to have to deal with the emotions that came along with that soon enough, and I was dreading it. But there were other things that needed tending to as well. Things I felt more sure of with every passing minute.

Clicking open the first message, I listened as my mother's voice poured through the speaker. *"Charlotte, sweetie, you missed your appointment with the doctor yesterday. You do know it's very hard to get appointments like those at such short notice. I'll reschedule, but you should know what an awful imposition this is."* The message clicked off.

No "I love you," no "I hope you're safe." Again, no question about where I was. For them, it was all about damage control.

Well, I was sick of being a liability. With shaking fingers, I dialed my mother's number and waited until her bored, upper-crust tones filled the line.

"Charlotte, finally."

"Hello, Mother."

"What day will work well for the doctor? I assume you got my message?"

"I'm not going to any doctor." My voice was more resolute than I'd ever heard it, and I straightened my shoulders to project even more.

"What on earth do you mean?" my mother cried. "You've had a nervous breakdown. You have to see a doctor to set you right."

"Nothing is wrong with me." I pulled my black credit card from my purse and gripped the scissors I'd found in Valentina's kitchen in one shaky hand. "Look, I was calling to let you know that I'm safe. Also, you should contact American Express and take my name off the account. I cut up my card."

"You did what?" she gasped.

"I've been thinking, and I want to earn what I get. Maybe Dad was right—about marketing and everything. I shouldn't walk into a job, but I also shouldn't walk into a car and a credit card either just because of who I was born to."

Holding the phone pinched between my cheek and shoulder, I snipped the card in half, then let out a satisfied sigh, feeling the strings of my puppeteer falling away. "I have enough to get by for a while. In the meantime, I'll find a new job, but I can't take any more of your money."

Silence reigned on the line for a long moment. When my mother spoke again, it was slowly and carefully, as if she were speaking to a deranged person. "Honey, is this some sort of Walden thing? Are you trying to—I don't know—only keep what brings you joy? Because I've read that book, and—"

"This isn't anything I got from a book. This is something I feel deep down inside," I said. "I just wanted to let you know."

"We only wanted to help you."

"I appreciate that, Mother. But I need to help myself now."

I didn't say all the rest burning in my throat. That everything I'd been given came with strings, and that I'd suddenly never felt freer. That their help was just a form of control. What would the point be? It would only hurt her. She loved me the best she knew how, and I'd been a willing participant, happy to take what they gave until now. No point in beating it to death. We'd all made mistakes. The key was to move forward as a better me, and hope that didn't destroy my relationship with my parents.

I ended the call despite her renewed cries for me to see a therapist anyway.

When I emerged from the bedroom, Valentina gave me a smile so big and wide that for the first time since I'd left Luke, I almost felt happy.

"We'll start looking for jobs for you next week," Valentina cried, "but for tonight? We're going to celebrate."

She popped the cork of a bottle of champagne. Foam sprayed the living room but she didn't care, she only let out a whoop of celebration. I joined her, laughing as the suds dripped onto the floor.

"Okay," I said. "It's time to get our party on."

We raided Valentina's closet and downed the champagne, then took an Uber to a nearby club. It should have been freeing—a perfect night of dancing and celebrating the way I'd always loved to do in New York.

But now? Now I could only look around and picture that going-away party at the little bar, how everyone knew each other, and how I was now surrounded by strangers who didn't know me any more than they cared about me—which was to say not at all.

An hour into the festivities, I tapped Valentina on the shoulder. "I think I'd like to head out. You can stay if you want."

She frowned. "You okay?"

"Yeah," I lied. "Just still tired from the trip."

She insisted on leaving with me, but she didn't press for answers. I felt nothing but relief as I climbed into bed and pulled the covers over my head a half hour later.

I'd taken a huge step with my parents, and that had felt amazing. But once the euphoria had faded, I realized I still had a gaping hole in my heart.

And the only person who could fill it was more than a thousand miles away.

Chapter Twenty-Six

Luke

Another few days passed and I worked even harder, throwing myself into the distillery with everything I had. Business was booming, and the regular order from the bar had doubled in the span of a week. Occasionally, Duke or Molly would stop by to see what was going on—and to talk to me yet again about Charlotte—but for the most part, this was my baby. My big chance to make a difference.

Still, every night I pulled out my phone and did what was quickly becoming a ritual. I opened Facebook, Instagram, and Twitter, searching for any mention of Charlotte, but Molly was right. Charlotte hadn't posted anything since the day before she left.

The only way to know she was okay would be to call her.

To ask how she was doing.

To beg her to come back.

I took a deep breath. For days, this decision had been

looming over me. I thought again about my mother, trapped in a marriage that didn't work. I thought about Sarah, who, despite all her positive qualities, hadn't come to Shady Grove for the right reasons. I'd begged them both to stay when they'd already made up their minds to leave, and Charlotte . . .

Wasn't she the one who'd wanted me to ask her to stay? Wasn't her asking me an indication that she needed my validation—some proof that I really, truly wanted her here?

And I did.

More than anything, I wanted her here with me.

So, what the fuck are you doing moping around here, you idiot?

I whipped out my phone, and before I could let my own fears convince me to change my mind, booked myself a ticket to Los Angeles. It might never work out, but goddamn it, I was going to try.

Chapter Twenty-Seven

Charlotte

City life wasn't how I remembered it.

Within the first week of arriving in Los Angeles, I'd gotten myself a job as a barista and had made a couple of new friends who liked to party. But as much as I tried to fit in, something still stuck out like a sore thumb . . . and I was beginning to think that something was *me*.

My mother had called a few more times, trying to ensure I'd go see a doctor. My father had even called and insisted that if I'd only come back, I could work for his company after all.

But now that I'd had my awakening, their attempts didn't affect me the way they'd hoped. Instead, I listened to their concerns, considered everything they said, and hung up feeling even better about my decision than I had before.

And every single time, I'd wonder with a bittersweet pang if Luke would be proud of me.

Of course, that thought often led me down a dark

and dangerous path. Even looking at my phone nowadays had me scrolling through my contacts and double-checking my texts, just in case I'd missed a message.

But I knew I hadn't.

Luke hadn't posted on Facebook or Twitter, and he didn't have an Instagram account. I'd started a few posts of my own, talking about the wonderful sun and sand of California, but then deleted them and put away my phone. I wasn't going to lie to the world when I was already lying to myself.

California was beautiful and sunny and sandy, yes. But it was lonely, and the traffic sucked. All the buildings felt like big industrial blocks with no charm or character, nothing like the cute little shops along the main street of Shady Grove.

If Luke came to Los Angeles, all he would see was the thing he hated most—the ridiculous city-slicker nonsense that made him stay so firmly in Shady Grove to begin with. I was having a hard time admitting it, but I missed the warmth and charm of that little speck on the map.

When my latest shift at the nearby café ended, I hung up my apron and ducked under the counter, punching out quickly before I headed down the sidewalk and back to Valentina's place.

It was convenient—only a few blocks away—and when I approached, I found her putting something in my old-but-new-to-me clunker of a car. I'd sold my Audi the day after I cut up my credit cards, and still hadn't decided what to do with the money left over after I bought my clunker. My parents refused to accept the excess back since the car had been a graduation gift, but I knew I wasn't that person anymore. I felt like a fraud driving a car I hadn't paid for myself.

"What are you doing?" I asked.

She looked up at me, her eyes wide, reminding me of a cat that had been caught with its paw in the fishbowl. "Nothing."

"Come on, what's up?"

"Look, I'm just . . . I'm trying to help."

I rounded the car and peered inside to see my own purple suitcase in the backseat, alongside Valentina's bright orange one.

"What's going on?" I asked, a sizzle of apprehension running through me.

She offered me a hesitant smile. "Okay, so . . . we're going to Texas." She raised her hands and wiggled her fingers with a little squeal of excitement. "Surprise!"

Stunned, I stared at her. "We can't go to Texas, Val. It's a grueling drive. Which I know because I just drove it. And besides, I've got a job—"

"Oh, that?" she said with a dismissive wave of her hand. "I quit it for you."

"You what?" I shouted, my stomach pitching.

Valentina smiled a little wider. "Yeah, I called them a few minutes ago, pretending I was you, and told them today was your last shift because you had a sick relative out of town who needed you."

I blinked, unsure of what to even say to that.

"Oh, please, you hated that job, Charlotte. And if you want it so bad, they said they totally understood and you could come back anytime. Fact is, I'm sick of watching you sit around and mope. If what you and Luke have is *it*, like the real-deal true love? Then you need to make an effort for it."

"But what about what he wants?"

"Well, you're clearly not happy here, honey. Plus, you said you think he has a problem with women leaving. If you want to prove to him how different you are, going back would mean the world to him." Valentina shrugged. "Sounds simple enough to me. We can drive in shifts to shave some time off the trip, and when we get there, I'll find a hotel to shack up in and make a fun vacation of it. Come on, say yes."

I looked at the car and flattened my lips into a line as I tried not to let my excitement build. Just because I went back to Shady Grove didn't mean that Luke would want to see me once I got there.

That fear lodged in my throat, so instead I voiced another of my fears that made me a little less panicky. "Do you think this hunk of junk can even make it that far?"

"Only one way to find out. All you have to do is get in and drive."

I glanced from her to the steering wheel, thinking of the painful drive here. I hadn't seen any of the sweeping desert landscape or the pretty sunsets. I'd been too distracted by my tears and the ache in my chest. The chance to see it all again . . .

Hell, who was I kidding? The chance to see Luke again?

I'd give just about anything for that.

When I slid into the driver's seat, Valentina jumped for joy, literally hopped up and down before climbing in beside me, all smiles.

"You're my hero right now. Look at you, all badass and awesome and taking a risk. I'm so proud of you."

"Calm down," I said with a chuckle. "We're going to chase a boy. It's not like we discovered the cure for cancer."

To be honest, I was only playing it cool. If I had my way, I'd have done somersaults and cartwheels all down the street at the idea of seeing Luke again. This was who I wanted to be all along—a woman who knew what she wanted and grabbed life by the balls. I just needed a little shove from my bestie.

But what would Luke do when he saw me? What would he say?

Jesus, what if I got there and he wasn't alone? Could he have found another girl in the week that I'd been gone?

Dread coiled through me at that thought, and Valentina and I discussed it at length over the next several hours, along with my speech for Luke once we arrived. We laughed and talked about what we'd do when we got to Shady Grove, and I promised her a day trip to Austin since she'd sacrificed so much for my love life.

•••

Two days later, my heart started pounding as I drove through San Antonio.

Valentina woke up from her nap, rubbing her eyes as she blinked up at me. "Are we getting close?" she asked, her voice still husky from sleep.

"Yup." My palms suddenly slick, I swiped one hand on my shorts.

I'd been so focused on how right things could go when I saw Luke again, I hadn't really considered the alternative. It was only sinking in now that if he rejected me, I could be making the return drive tomorrow ... completely heartsick. Vacation plan or no, there was no way I could stay in Shady Grove if Luke didn't want me there. Every single inch of that town was a searing reminder of our time together. Staying there would be like pouring salt in a wound over and over again.

I sucked in a steadying breath and shot her a tight smile. "Almost there."

"What are you going to do when you see him?" she asked, her drowsiness fading as she got that rah-rah life-coach look in her eyes.

"I'm ..." I let out a deep sigh, trying to push out all my fears and negative feelings along with it. "I'm going to tell him that I'm not asking him for any promises; I'm just asking for a chance. That I'm going to stay and give this a try, and that no matter what he thinks based on his ex's behavior, I know this can work. I'm going to tell him that I haven't been the same without him, and that . . ."

"That?" she prompted me when I hesitated.

"I'm going to tell him that I love him." I groaned and squeezed the wheel more tightly. "It's crazy that we only spent a week together, but I fell hard and fast. I can't go on without knowing I gave this a fair shake."

"That's my girl." Valentina gave me an approving nod.

I practiced my little speech all the way down the interstate until I finally took the exit that led into Shady Grove. From there, the trip to the Wilder property was quick and easy. My heart thundered as I took the turn for the distillery, and when I reached the end of the road, my heart stopped beating altogether.

Not because I saw Luke, although that would have done it.

Nope, my normal bodily functions had ceased because I was certain the Mercedes parked in the little visitor lot next to the barn belonged to none other than one Prescott Billingsley the Sixth.

Dear God, what the hell is happening?

Chapter Twenty-Eight

Luke

"You can't be serious," I said, shaking my head in disbelief.

The other man nodded, then tipped his glass to me. "Pardon my language, but it's been nothing short of a fucking disaster. Her parents are calling me every day asking if I've heard from her, and she's not picking up her damned phone. It's been a total shit show."

"To be left at the altar like that, though." I let out a low whistle of sympathy.

I thought it had been bad to have an engagement ring returned to me. But to have all my friends and family see me get dumped on what was supposed to be the happiest day of my life? I could hardly imagine.

Worse yet, I couldn't figure out why a woman would leave him. He was a decent-looking guy with sandy hair and nice, kind eyes. If he was looking to invest in someone else's business, he was clearly well off and good with his money. In the few moments we'd spent together, he'd even cracked a joke or two.

I guess that just goes to show you. You never know what can happen in this life.

After the last week, I should have known that better than anyone. I'd barely slept a wink since Charlotte left me, and I'd known she was leaving. All I could think of was getting close to her again. Imagine this poor guy with his fiancée jilting him like that when he'd planned on forever with her? She must have been a real piece of work.

"Sorry, buddy. That sounds really tough." I touched my glass to his again and we both took another sip. "I can totally understand why you'd be throwing yourself back into business then. Jesus, man," I said, shaking my head in quiet commiseration.

"Actually, that's only part of the reason for my visit." He leaned in with a sigh. "I'm looking for someone."

The floorboards creaked behind us and I turned in my chair, expecting to see Duke stroll in. What I saw made me nearly cough up the burning liquid sliding down my throat.

"Charlotte," I sputtered.

Then I realized I hadn't been the only one. The man next to me had said her name at exactly the same time. I glanced at him and turned back to Charlotte to find her gaping at him.

"What's going on?" I asked, my surprise and joy at seeing her tempered by total and complete confusion.

"Speak of the devil," he murmured, and Charlotte's eyebrows inched higher.

Behind her, a slim woman with thick, dark hair edged into the room and held up a hand, waving to me shyly. "Hey," she said in a voice richer than I'd expected. "I'm Valentina. And you must be Luke."

"Uh, hi," I said. "Maybe you could explain—"

Charlotte stalked toward the man beside me and finally seemed to find her voice. "What the hell are you doing here?"

"Look, you might have left me but that doesn't mean I stopped caring. You posted on Instagram, so I did some—"

"Snooping," she spat out, cutting in.

"Research," he said, correcting her, "and I came here to make sure you're okay. Which, obviously, you are."

This time, his eyes found mine and something clicked.

"Speak of the devil."

I scrubbed a hand over my face and stood from my bar stool. "The girl you were talking about is Charlotte?" I asked, and he gave me a clipped nod. "I thought you were an investor—"

Charlotte let out a humorless laugh. "So, you lied to him to get to me? That's low, Prescott. Who put you up to this? My parents?"

"You said your name was Scott," I muttered, my gut clenching in shock.

Prescott? Prescott Billingsley was the guy sitting next to me—the guy who had apparently been nothing to write home about? Except that wasn't true either, because she'd been fucking engaged to the guy. The whole time she'd been here, she'd been *engaged*. And she'd left him high and dry, just like Sarah had done to me. Worse than that,

Charlotte had lied to me.

"I use the name in business so there's no confusion. My father is named Prescott as well. And nobody put me up to anything." He shook his head, then glanced at me. "I'm sorry. I hadn't had a chance to explain, and I've never turned down a free glass of whiskey, which—considering you know Charlotte—I'm sure you can understand."

My head spun again as twin urges warred inside me—one to knock this guy's fucking head off for talking about my woman like that, and the other to tear my hair out at the lunacy of this situation.

"What the fuck is going on, Charlotte?" I shouted.

The whole time she'd been here, she'd been hiding. Hiding from Prescott and from her parents, and lying to me and my family about why she was here. She obviously hadn't felt that she could trust me, that she didn't know me well enough to confide in me. And here I'd bought a ticket to go to her and try to make this work.

Honestly, I wasn't sure which part of it stung the most.

Little snippets of memories played through my mind—the way she'd snapped at me when I'd pressed her about her ex, how angry she'd been when she'd slammed down her phone in my kitchen, the way she always looked at her cell like it was about to detonate at any moment.

"Nothing to write home about?" I asked quietly, and then forced myself to look at her, wondering if I'd ever be able to do that again without feeling sick.

Charlotte's gaze darted between Prescott and me, her eyes brimming with tears. "You have to understand—"

I wasn't interested in hearing it. I turned on Prescott, now remembering the things he'd told me before she walked through the door. He'd talked about what a pain in the ass his fiancée had been. How he didn't love her. How he'd only gone after her to make sure she cleaned up her own mess back home before moving on with her life like nothing had happened.

"What the fuck is wrong with you?" I demanded, my hands balled into fists at my side.

Prescott's eyes narrowed. "What the fuck is wrong with me? What's wrong with you?"

"You couldn't just leave her the fuck alone?" I growled. "You didn't think she'd been through enough?"

"Ah." Prescott nodded. "So that's how you know each other."

"And what's that supposed to mean?"

"I mean you fucked her. Not to put too fine a point on it," he muttered.

All I had to do was swing. One punch and he'd be on the floor—that was the one advantage of growing up without having money to fix all my problems, I supposed. But he was smaller than me, obviously just as confused, and the fight wouldn't have been a fair one.

No matter how much I wanted to teach him a fucking lesson.

"Don't talk about her like that. Or better yet, how about you don't talk about her at all?" I started, but then Charlotte's hand was on my chest, pushing me back toward the bar.

"Look, I couldn't tell you," she said, her eyes pleading. Then she turned to Prescott. "You didn't have to come here and do this to me."

"Do this to you?" This time it was his turn to let out a humorless laugh. "Do you have any idea what I've been dealing with? Your parents are all over me, and I had to handle the fallout of your big break for freedom. The least you could've done was return my calls."

She shook her head, her hand still pressed to my chest as she replied to him. "I didn't want you to try to convince me to change my mind," she whispered miserably.

"Change your mind?" Prescott shook his head. "I don't want you back. Your leaving was the best thing that ever happened to me. You set us both free. I realized that two seconds after you left, when I found I felt nothing but surprise and relief. But I can't handle the fallout on my own. You might not love me, Charlotte, but I know you care. Just help me deal with this mess and our families." He raked a hand through his hair and groaned. "Do you have any idea what our mothers are putting me through?"

A single tear slid down her cheek. "I didn't hurt

you?"

Prescott shook his head. "My pride was wounded and I was pissed, don't get me wrong, but I don't love you. We weren't right for each other, and never have been. The family pressure was just too strong for me to see that."

"I—" she started, but I sidestepped her and made my way for the barn door.

"Well, I'm glad you guys have worked everything out. Have a good time in New York. And lock up on your way out."

I shoved the door open and scanned my surroundings for anything I could hit, something that might relieve the pressure building inside me, about to blow. Because all that time, Charlotte had been lying to me. All that fucking time.

Fuck, runaways must have been able to smell me from a mile away. First my mother and then Sarah, and now Charlotte too.

"Luke!"

Charlotte shouted to me from the barn door but I was already too far away, and her voice was nearly drowned out by the whipping of the wind.

I had to get back home, needed to try to return my ticket to LA and move on.

A little voice inside me laughed. *Move on to what, Luke? The next fucking tumbleweed that rolls into your life and back out of it?*

God, how could I have been so stupid?

Maybe I should have gone back to shake Prescott Billingsley the Sixth's hand. I might have a broken heart, but he might have just saved me from total annihilation.

Chapter Twenty-Nine

Charlotte

The wind whipped my hair over my face as I called for Luke again, but he didn't stop walking. In fact, he didn't even bother to turn around.

Part of me wanted to run the other way. Admit defeat and accept that I'd done this to myself and deserved whatever happened next. But the other part was so damned mad at him that nothing else mattered anymore.

Whatever happened, he needed to hear the truth from my lips. If he still hated me, so be it. At least I could go on and try to piece some semblance of a life together with no regrets.

I took one step forward, then stopped as a big blue truck rolled into the parking area and stopped next to my sedan. Duke climbed from the driver's seat and blinked at me, although he seemed much less surprised to see me than his brother had.

"What's the deal? I heard there was a investor here?" He glanced from me to the other cars and then gave me a confused look. "And where the hell did you come from?"

"It's a long story," I said.

The wind picked up again as Valentina tripped through the door to join me. She stared from Duke to me and back again.

"Oh, sorry, I'll just—" She tried to move, but then stopped. "Wait, you weren't wearing—"

"This is Duke." I nodded toward him. "Luke's twin brother. Luke's gone," I murmured, my throat sticking on the words.

"Hey there," Valentina said with a smile, and wrinkled her nose when Duke tipped the bill of his ball cap toward her. "Charlotte, Prescott says he still wants to talk to you."

"Does it have to be this moment? Surely he realizes I'm a little busy right now?" I asked her, staring in Luke's wake.

"Yes, now would be good, Charlotte." This time it was Prescott who spoke, poking his head out from behind the barn door.

I let out a sigh and turned to face him. "I'm so sorry for what I did to you. It was immature and selfish, and you deserved better. I'm happy to do whatever it takes to clean up the mess with our parents the second I'm done here, okay? I just need a few minutes with Luke. He wasn't part of any of this, and he's got so much going on here, trying to get this business—"

"That's what I wanted to tell you before I got out of your hair," he said with a half smile. "I'm not mad anymore. I think I was just worried, and now that I've seen you . . ." He gestured around with a little laugh. "Now that I've seen you with all this and him, it makes weird sense to me. I get it. Oddly enough, I think you belong here. What I wanted to tell you was that I'd like to invest in the distillery. After you and Luke talk, I'd appreciate it if you would give him my number and ask him to give me a call."

"What?" I blinked at him in surprise. "You don't have to do that. You've done nothing wrong here, and—"

"Believe me, I know that. But I tried your . . . friend's liquor, and I like it. He's got something special that I think is a worthwhile investment. Him, this place . . . it's got a whole vibe to it that I think can be a huge moneymaker. So, when you work everything out, let him know that I'll be in touch." He shoved his hands in his pockets and nodded to Valentina. "Val."

She looked from Prescott to Duke, apparently unsure of who was on what side, and if she should be mad at someone or not.

"Thanks, Prescott," I said sincerely, the lump in my throat growing. Whatever happened, his belief in Luke's business made me so frigging proud, I could burst. "You're a good man."

"And you don't need to come back. I'll handle things in New York. I mostly just came here to make sure you were okay, because they were starting to get to me. Your mother even mentioned a cult?" He laughed and shook his head. "Anyway, you're clearly fine."

"If you need anything, please let me know. I don't want to leave you holding the bag. That was never my intention."

"If I need you, I'll call." He nodded again and waved a good-bye to the others before climbing into his car and driving away.

I watched him go, then turned back to Valentina and Duke, who were both staring at me. "I have to go find Luke."

My heart pounded again in panic as I imagined the kind of head start he'd managed. When I moved for my car, Duke held up a hand.

"In that?" He pointed to my beat-up clunker with a wince. "Is it even street legal? Where did you get that thing, a junkyard?"

I rolled my eyes and yanked open the door. "Val, will you entertain Duke here and fill him in on everything?"

"That sounds like something I could get behind," Duke said, his eyes alight.

Valentina's lips quirked into a smile. "Yeah, sure. Come on, you can pour me a drink," she said, and led him into the barn.

I slipped behind the wheel and sped off for the farmhouse. It was the obvious choice, but Luke simply had to be there. If he wasn't . . .

Then I'd wait. He'd have to come home sometime. I'd left once before without telling him how I felt, and I wasn't going to do it again.

• • •

I needn't have worried. When I pulled up at his house, it was to find the front door open and the hall light on.

"Luke!"

I shouted his name and rushed into the house before he could slam the door in my face and lock it. I called his name again, searching the living room and then the kitchen. At last, I found him behind the old-fashioned desk in his office.

"You don't want to do this, Charlotte," he said without looking up. He was hunched over in the chair, apparently examining a few of the branding designs we'd come up with.

"Do what? Drive day and night to get here and have you ignore me?" I shot back. "Yep, you're right about that one, and yet here I am."

He didn't look up. "You should go back to New York with your husband."

"He's . . . he's not my husband," I stammered, my hands starting to shake at the icy chill in his voice.

"Only because you got cold feet and left him at the altar," Luke muttered.

"No. We're not married because we weren't meant to be, and I was smart enough to see it before it was too late." I stalked toward the desk and swiped my hand over the top of it, sending the papers flying into the air.

As they floated to the floor like confetti, Luke sputtered, "What the—"

When he finally looked up, I grabbed his chin, forcing him to meet my gaze as I pleaded, "Listen to me."

His lips thinned into a resolute line, but he didn't pull away.

"I couldn't tell you about him. At first, I thought I was in town for so short a time that it wouldn't matter, and then, well, I was running away. I didn't want to talk about him with anyone, let alone with you. Don't you see?

I needed some time to process it all. At least give me the chance to tell you the whole story now. And if, once I've finished, you still want me to leave, then I will."

I released Luke's chin but he just looked at me, silently waiting for me to go on.

I started in a rush before he changed his mind. "Prescott and I met at a charity function at our parents' country club. He bought a date with me at one of those stupid bachelorette auctions."

Luke's mouth twisted, but he didn't say anything.

"I later found out that our parents had arranged things that way. We traveled in the same circles, so the more I saw him, the more it seemed to . . . I don't know, work. After my dad refused to let me into the family business, I thought I needed a man to support me because I wasn't talented enough, and Prescott was okay with that. We got along fine and we're friends, but . . . I never loved him. We never even slept together. I only agreed to marry him because I knew what was expected of me, but when I put on that wedding dress at the church and saw myself in it, I felt nothing."

I shook my head, remembering the bone-chilling calm I'd felt that day.

"If I could have called it off before that moment—if I could have realized what kind of mistake I was making—I would never have left him that way. It was an awful thing to do. But I didn't realize until then, and I can't feel bad for not waltzing into a marriage that I didn't want. I couldn't bear to think of living my whole life without ever feeling . . . well, without ever feeling the way I feel about you."

Silence hung between us and I waited for Luke to say something, anything. But he didn't. He just stared at me, studying me with an inscrutable expression.

"I didn't want to love you, you know," I told him. "It doesn't make any sense to spend one week with someone and fall so deeply in love that you can't go on with your life the way you'd planned, but when I got to the city, all I could think about was you. I didn't want to go to parties with strangers. I wanted to sit around a picnic table with your family and drink whiskey and just . . . live. Have family dinners. Lie in your bed all night just talking to you."

I chewed hard on my bottom lip. "I came here to tell you that. It felt like something you should know, but I don't need you to ask me to stay. Because no matter what you do, I'm staying here. I wasn't going to. If you didn't want me, I was going to turn tail and leave. But you know what? I love it here. And I love you. If you want me to leave, you're going to have to call the sheriff to get me out, you understand?"

Those cool green eyes of his drifted over me again, and he tipped his head in a single nod. "What if you change your mind like you did about Prescott? What if you wake up one day and realize that this wasn't what you really wanted?"

It was a fair question, but damn, did it cut deep.

I took his hand in mine and held it tightly, trying my best not to burst into tears. "Because this is the first time in my life I ever knew anything for sure. I know it down to the bottom of my soul, and that's not going to change. There are no guarantees in life; you know that. You could decide tomorrow that I'm not the one for you too. But guess what? I know that this . . . what we have? It's worth the risk. Take the leap with me, Luke. I won't let you down."

He was quiet for so long, I thought it was over. I'd lost. But then his hand tightened on mine and he pulled me onto his lap with a groan.

"Every day since you left," he said, "I've felt like an idiot. I think about you all the time—I'm surrounded by your ideas and your brilliance. You saved my family and the distillery, and . . . me. I need you to stay with me. I'm begging you to stay, because I love you. I was wrong to react the way I did, and I'm sorry, baby. If you ever need to run again, just promise this time that you'll take me with you."

I blinked hard, and he kissed the tear now sliding down my cheek. His mouth moved lower as he took my bottom lip between his, sucking on the tender skin. My tongue swept out to meet his as I trembled with joy and relief.

It was okay. We were going to be okay.

It might have been an instant or an hour before he broke our kiss, but when he did, I cleared my throat and grinned.

"I have some more good news for you too," I said.

"I've already got the best news in the world." He kissed my forehead. "You're here."

"Fine, then I won't tell you," I teased, and he gave me a little shake. "Okay, okay. You have two new investors for the distillery."

"I do?" He raised his eyebrows.

"Prescott wants in."

Luke looked conflicted about that for a moment. "And the other?"

"I sold my car. It's not much, but I do have a little money to play with. I was hoping I could come on as part of the team?"

"You want to invest in the distillery," he said slowly, as if he couldn't believe it.

"Of course I do. I believe in you."

Luke swept me up into another heart-stopping kiss. "Dammit, I love you," he whispered as he cupped my cheek. "Don't ever leave me again, duchess."

"I never, ever will."

Epilogue

Charlotte

Six months later

It didn't take me long to get my big fancy car back.

It wasn't a brand-new model, hadn't even been made in the last five years, but it was mine. And even better?

This time, I had earned it.

Today, it was dolled up with Just Married in white paint on the back window, and streamers and cans tied to the bumper.

From a window in the back room of the barn we'd been dressing in, I looked out at it as I smiled to myself, knowing what my parents would think when they finally arrived. But then again, I was getting better about not caring when my mom did her best to wrinkle her Botoxed nose, or when my father tried to slide me a credit card I didn't need.

They meant well. They were just trying to take care of me in their own way.

But I could take care of myself now. And when I couldn't? Well, that's what Luke was for. He had my back and I had his.

Valentina opened the door that led outside, her hands filled with wildflowers. Since they sprang up like weeds all over the farm, I hadn't bothered to buy any bouquets.

"Oh!" Molly squealed from behind me. "Are we putting those in our hair?"

"I don't see why not." Valentina shrugged and glanced at me for approval.

I smiled. "Don't look at me. I don't care what you do with your hair."

Molly snatched up a few bright pink and yellow blooms, then rushed to the mirror and tucked them into the elaborate braid circling her head. I had to admit, the colors went well with the blush-colored bridesmaid dresses.

"I got some white ones too," Valentina said.

Molly turned around, grinning at me as Valentina

stepped close and adjusted my veil. Gently, she tucked the sprigs in a halo-like crown all around the tulle. When she finished, I looked in the mirror and my breath caught.

It couldn't have felt any more different from my first wedding.

Looking at myself wearing the pretty antique-lace gown and with simple wildflowers in my hair . . . I felt like myself. Like I'd finally found where I belonged.

And like I was about to enter into the best, most amazing journey of my life.

"So, explain to me again who we're walking down the aisle with?" Valentina asked.

"Molly's walking alone. And you're walking with Duke," I said for what felt like the millionth time.

Ever since the rehearsal dinner the night before, this seemed to be a point Valentina just couldn't get through her head . . . or rather, *wouldn't* get through her head.

"But Molly and Duke are siblings. Shouldn't they walk together?" Valentina asked. "Oh, or we could do a three-person sort of sandwich setup."

I rolled my eyes. "I don't think you'd all fit down the aisle like that. You're the maid of honor and he's the best man—you walk together. What's so scary about walking down the aisle with Duke, anyway?"

"She likes him," Molly sang, a grin spreading across her face.

"Stop it. I do not. I . . ." Valentina searched for the words, but her face was already turning red. "He just makes me uncomfortable is all."

"Hmm." I nodded. "Right. Now, put some flowers in your hair. It's almost show time."

I could hear the buzz of conversion coming from outside, and knew that the whole town was out there waiting for us, for me. A shiver of nervousness ran through me. This wasn't only our first wedding here at the Wilder Farm, an event we desperately needed to go well, it was *my* wedding.

Molly came up behind me and put her arm around my shoulders. "You're going to be great up there. I just came from seeing my brother, and I've never seen anybody so—"

"Scared?" I offered.

"Happy," she said.

Music rang out from the local band that we'd hired, and I turned to find Valentina on my other side, sprigs of flowers laced through her hair. She handed a makeshift bouquet of wildflowers to Molly and kept the rest for herself.

"What about me?" I asked with a pout.

"Well . . ." Molly opened the door and beckoned, and Duke peered around the door frame with a giant bouquet of pink gerbera daisies and baby's breath in his hands.

"My brother said his bride had to have the best," he said with a wink.

I clutched the flowers and took a long, deep breath of their light springtime fragrance. A small card was tucked into the blooms and I snatched it out, reading the words quickly.

Knock 'em dead, duchess. I'll be up there waiting.

I smiled and tucked the card down the bodice of my dress for safekeeping. This was it—the big moment.

Molly and Valentina slipped from the room and I turned again, taking one last look in the mirror before the music changed, signaling my entrance. My father would be waiting outside the door for me, his arm outstretched, waiting to walk me toward the man of my dreams. Then Luke would be there at the gazebo with the minister, counting on me.

And he could count on me all he wanted.

Because when I got to his side? There was no chance of me going anywhere else in this whole wide world.

Moments later, we headed out, and three steps down the grassy path littered with flowers, my gaze met Luke's. A warm shiver raced over my skin as the emotion in his eyes hit me. I'd never seen him filled with such awe—or such sheer happiness. And I knew in that moment that our life together would be beautiful. I could envision it all—laughter, love, passion, babies, and all the sweet whiskey kisses I could handle.

For ever and ever.

Acknowledgments

I would like to say a big ol' country thank-you to author Elizabeth Lee for your guidance with this story. Thank you for providing some creative direction and only making fun of me a few times when I didn't know the proper terminology to use. You are a sweetheart! I'm blessed to call you a friend.

My team is everything to me, and I couldn't do this without you. I'd like to squeeze Danielle Sanchez, Pam Berehulke, and Alyssa Garcia. A big thank-you to Sarah Hansen and Sara Eirew, who provided the beautiful cover design and photography. This book cover is one of my favorites.

I wish I could give every single reader a tackle-hug! That is how grateful I am for you. I truly appreciate every review, read, and mention of my books.

Many thanks!

About the Author

A *New York Times*, *Wall Street Journal*, and *USA TODAY* bestselling author of more than two dozen titles, Kendall Ryan has sold over two million books, and her books have been translated into several languages in countries around the world. Her books have also appeared on the *New York Times* and *USA TODAY* bestseller list more than three dozen times. Ryan has been featured in publications such as *USA TODAY*, *Newsweek*, and *In Touch Magazine*. She lives in Texas with her husband and two sons.

Website: www.kendallryanbooks.com

Other Books by Kendall Ryan

Unravel Me
Make Me Yours
Working It
Craving Him
All or Nothing
When I Break Series
Filthy Beautiful Lies Series
The Gentleman Mentor
Sinfully Mine
Bait & Switch
Slow & Steady
The Room Mate
The Play Mate
The House Mate
The Bed Mate
The Soul Mate
Hard to Love
Reckless Love
Resisting Her
The Impact of You
Screwed
Monster Prick
The Fix Up

Printed in Great Britain
by Amazon